SIR LADYBUG

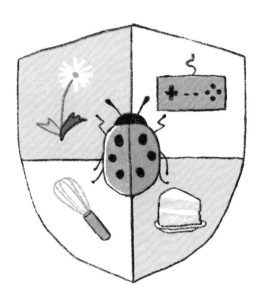

Corey R. Tabor

BALZER + BRAY

Imprints of HarperCollins Publishers

These bugs are for
Mandy and Will.

Special thanks to
Rebecca Sherman

HarperAlley is an imprint of HarperCollins Publishers.

Balzer + Bray is an imprint of HarperCollins Publishers.

Sir Ladybug
Copyright © 2022 by Corey R. Tabor
All rights reserved. Manufactured in Italy.
No part of this book may be used or reproduced in any manner whatsoever without written
permission except in the case of brief quotations embodied in critical articles and reviews.
For information address HarperCollins Children's Books, a division of HarperCollins Publishers,
195 Broadway, New York, NY 10007.
www.harpercollinschildrens.com

ISBN 978-0-06-306906-0

The art for this book was created digitally.
Typography by Dana Fritts and Corey R. Tabor
22 23 24 25 26   RTLO   10 9 8 7 6 5 4 3 2 1

First Edition

CONTENTS

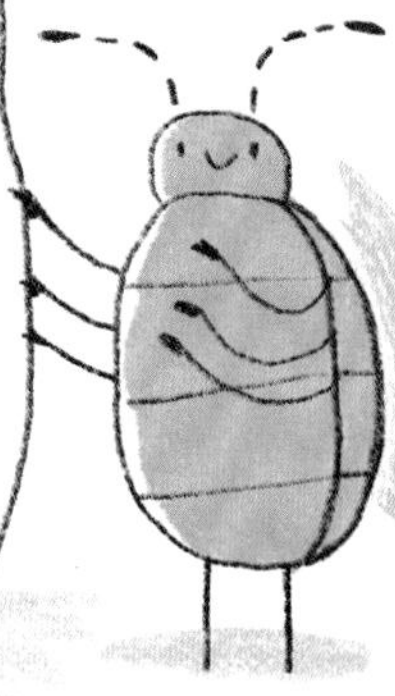

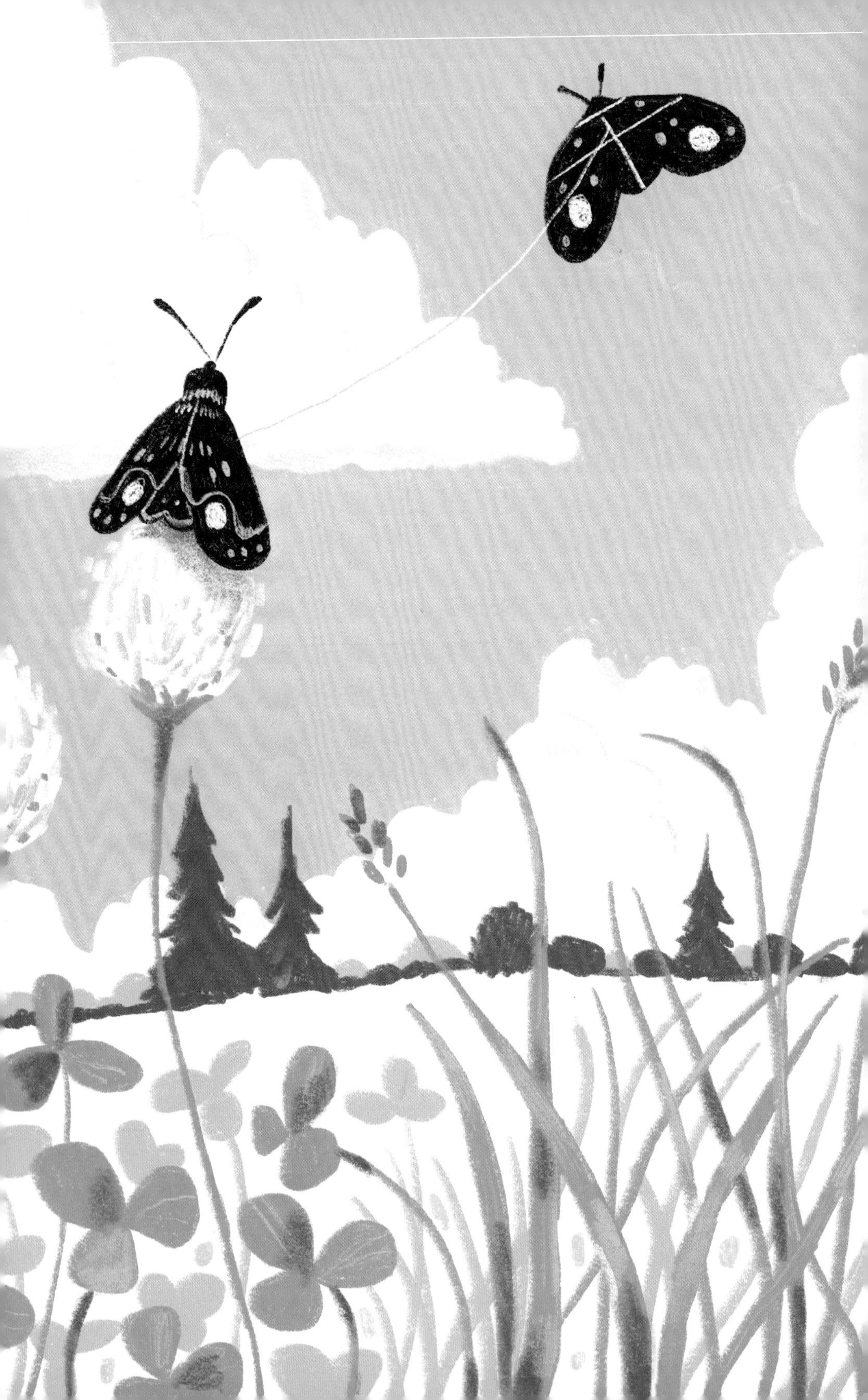

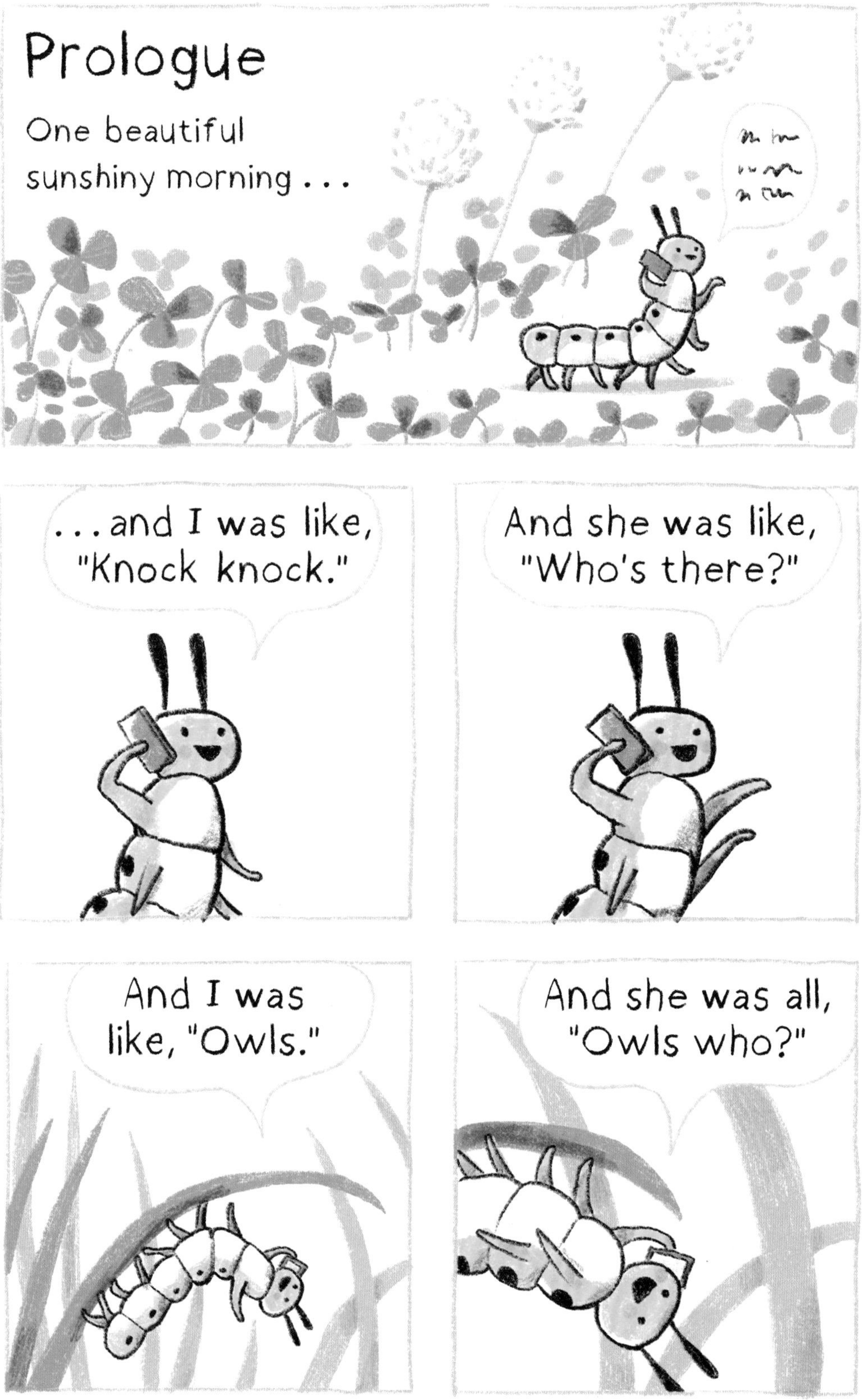
Prologue
One beautiful sunshiny morning . . .
. . . and I was like, "Knock knock."
And she was like, "Who's there?"
And I was like, "Owls."
And she was all, "Owls who?"

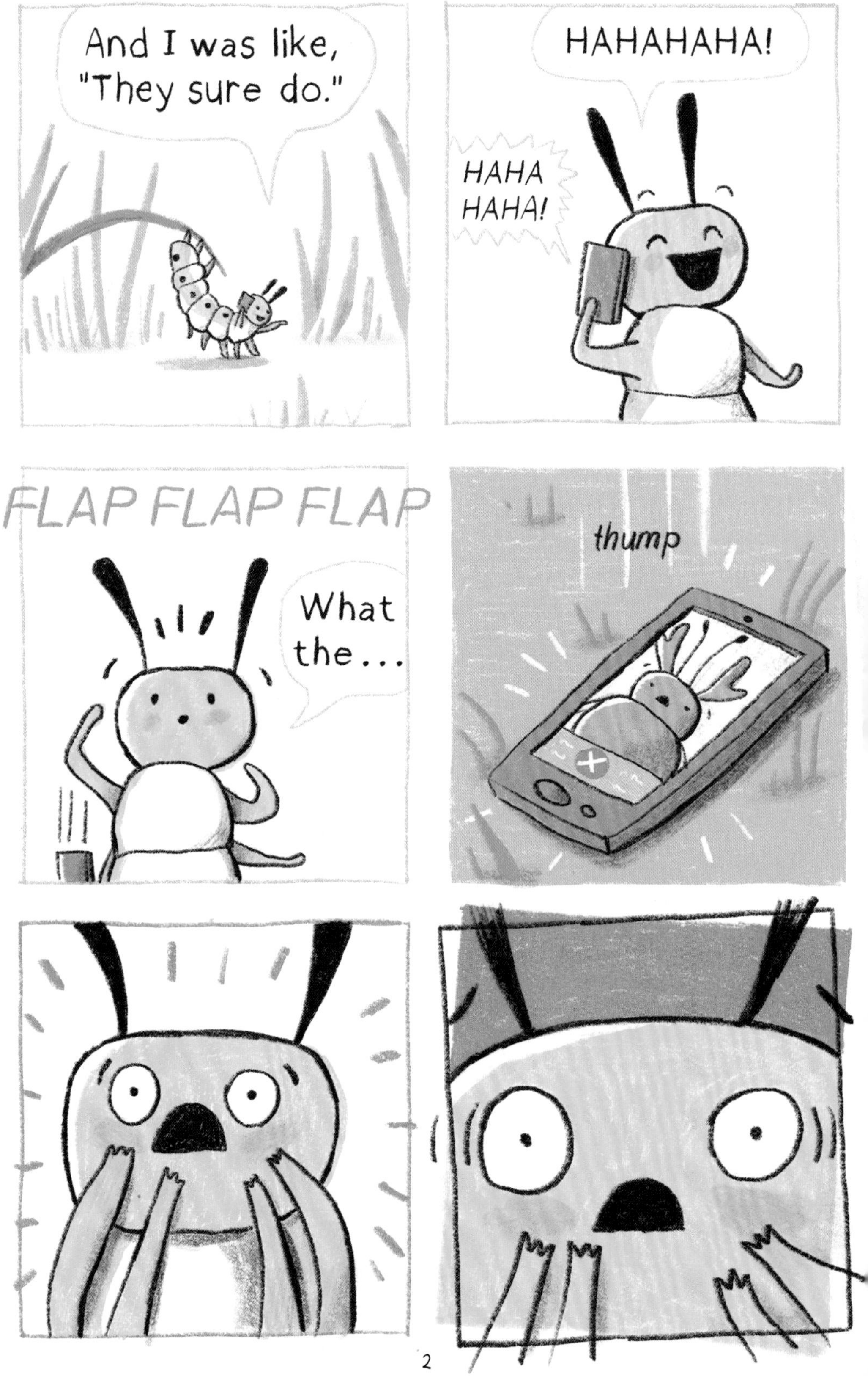
And I was like, "They sure do."
HAHAHAHA!
HAHA HAHA!
FLAP FLAP FLAP
What the...
thump

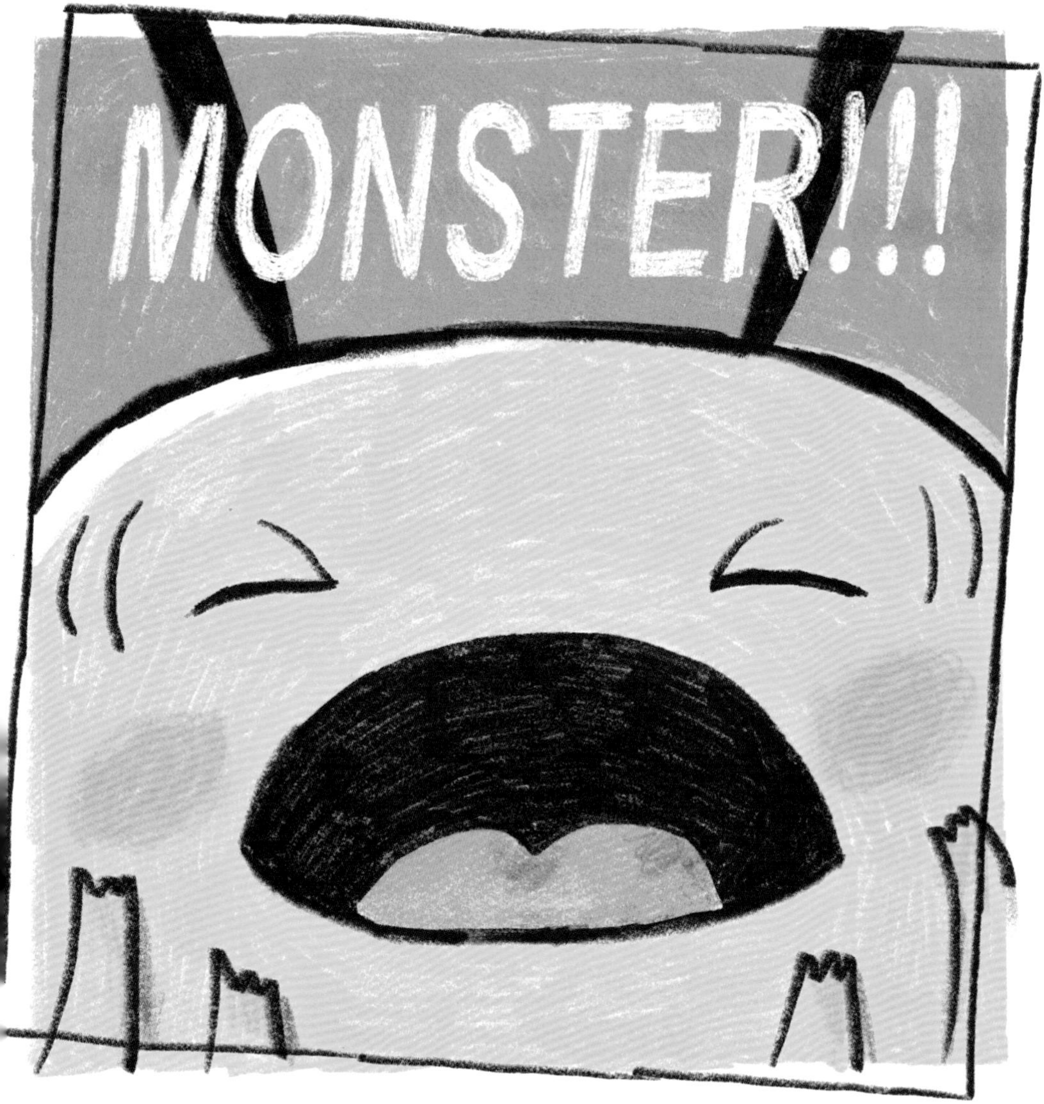
MONSTER!!!

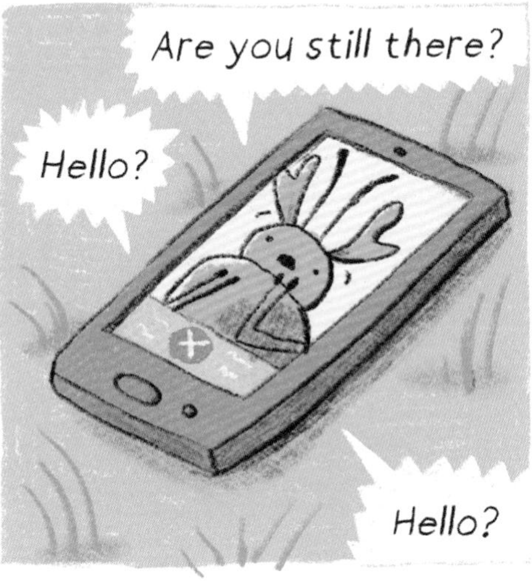
Are you still there?
Hello?
Hello?

Chapter 1: Introducing Sir Ladybug!

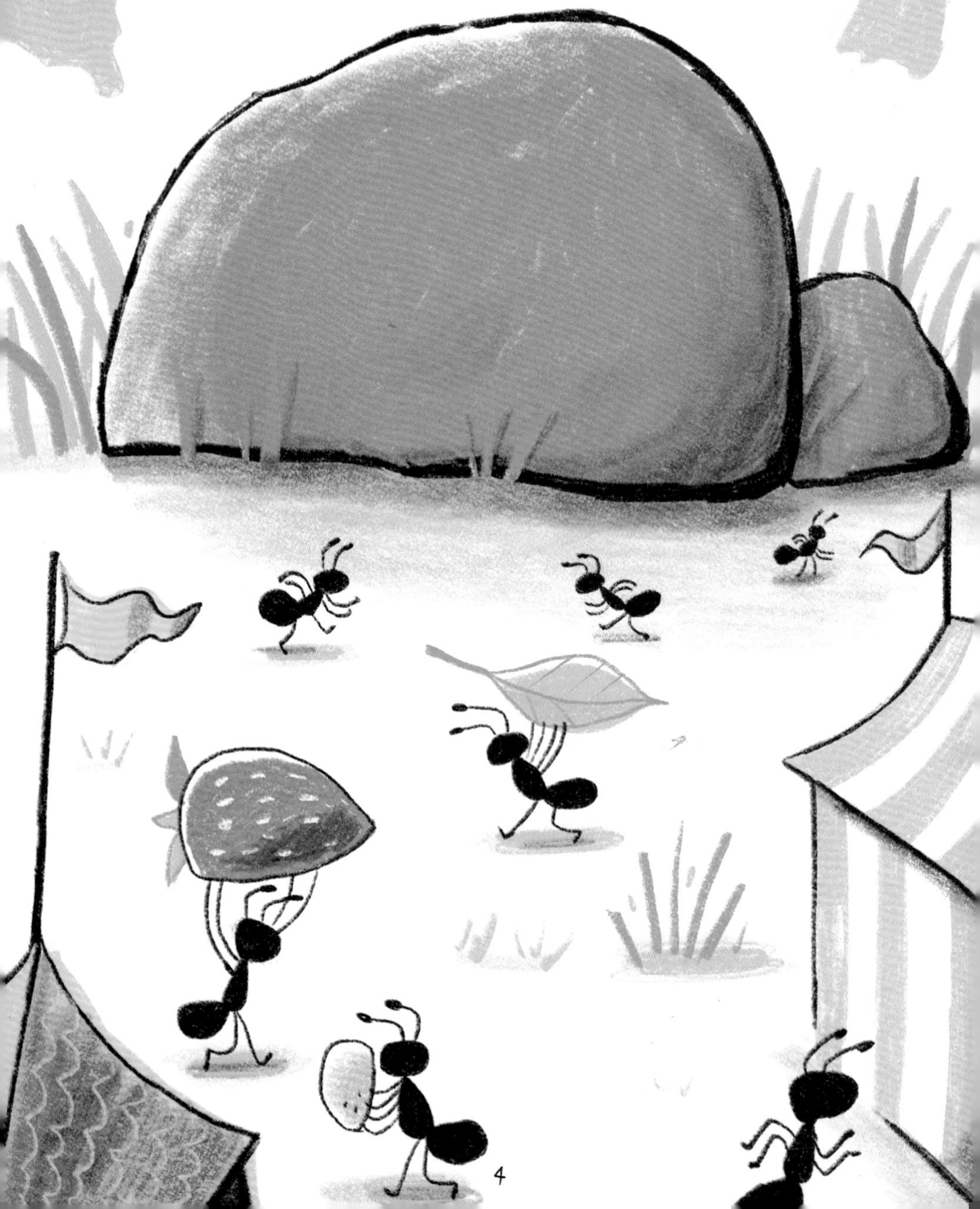

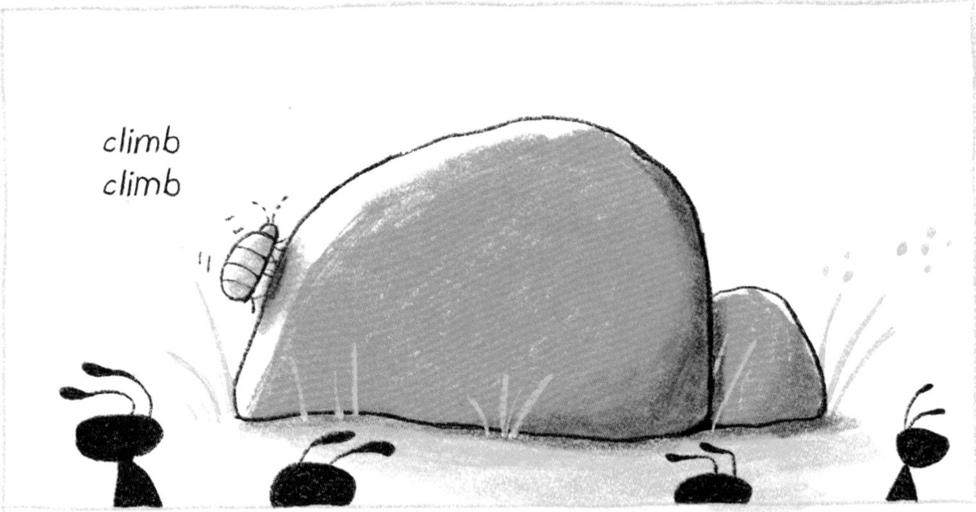
climb
climb

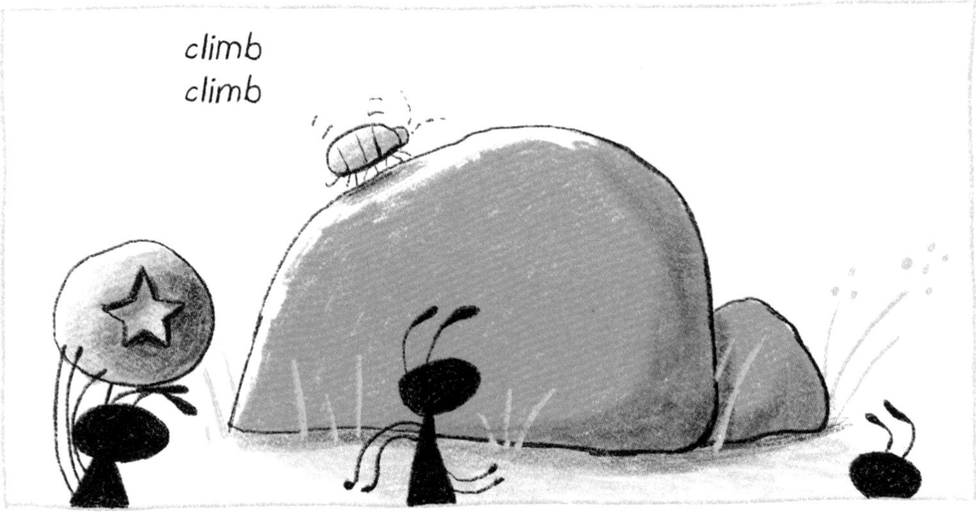
climb
climb

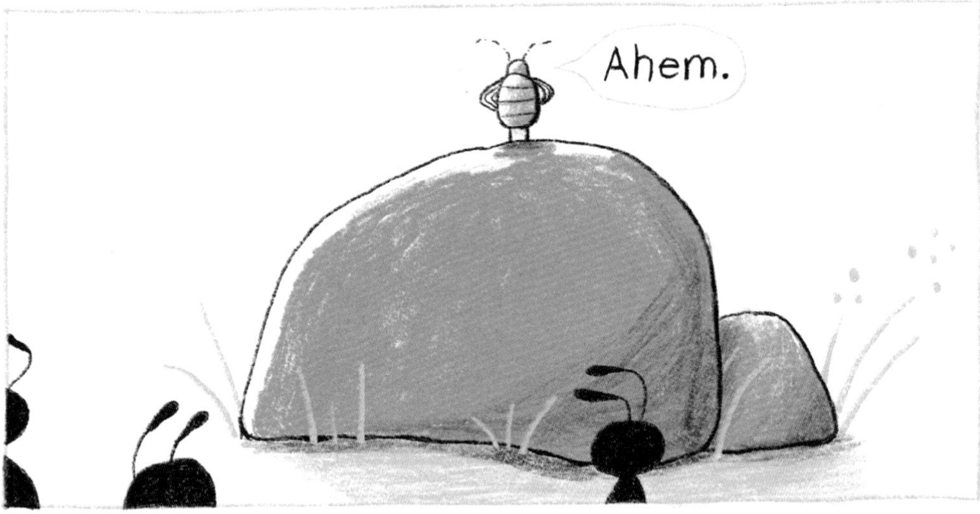
Ahem.

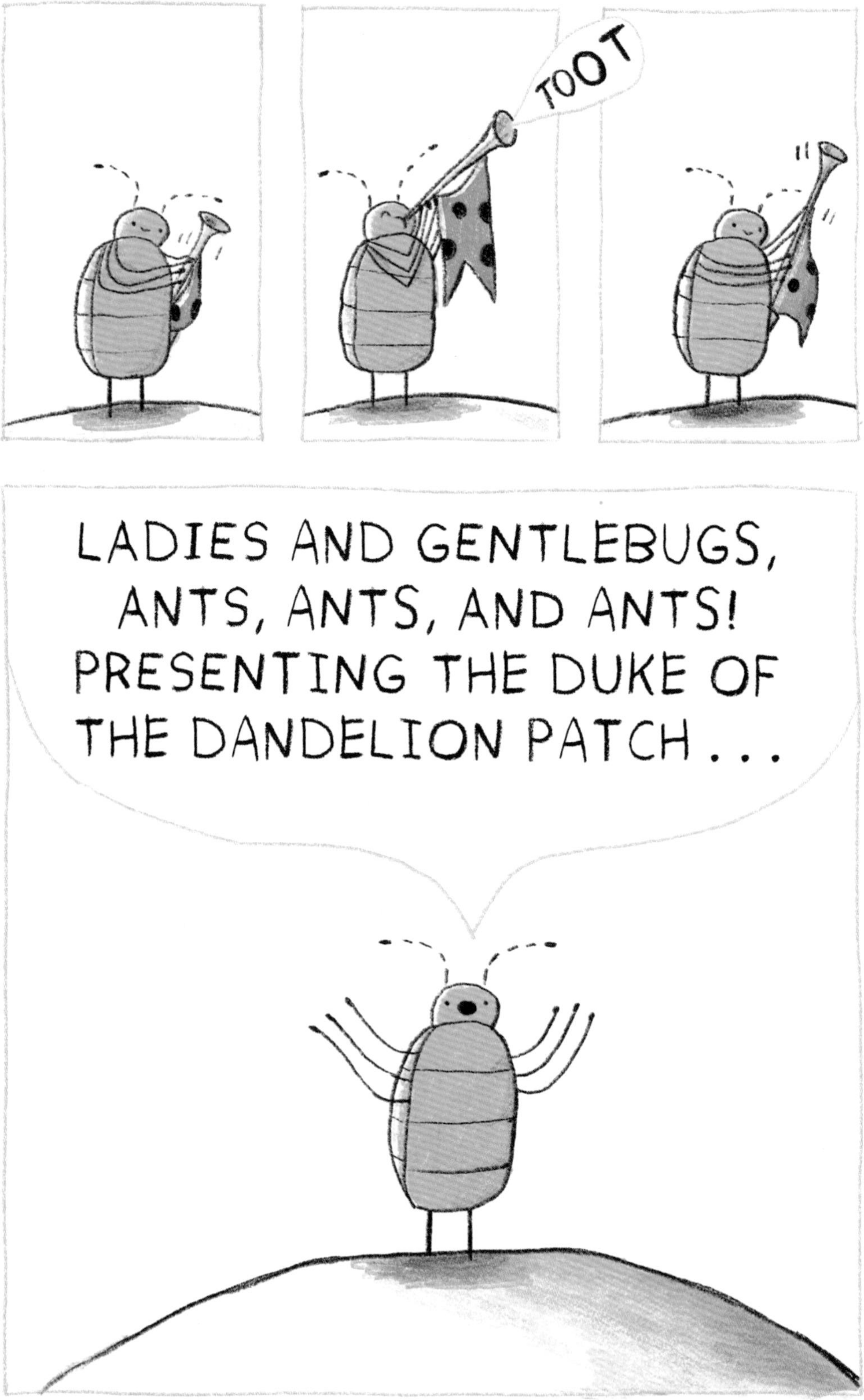
TOOT
LADIES AND GENTLEBUGS, ANTS, ANTS, AND ANTS! PRESENTING THE DUKE OF THE DANDELION PATCH . . .

... CHAMPION OF TRUTH AND JUSTICE ...

There you are, Pell! I was wondering where you ...

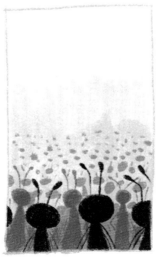

Oh, Pell. Not again.

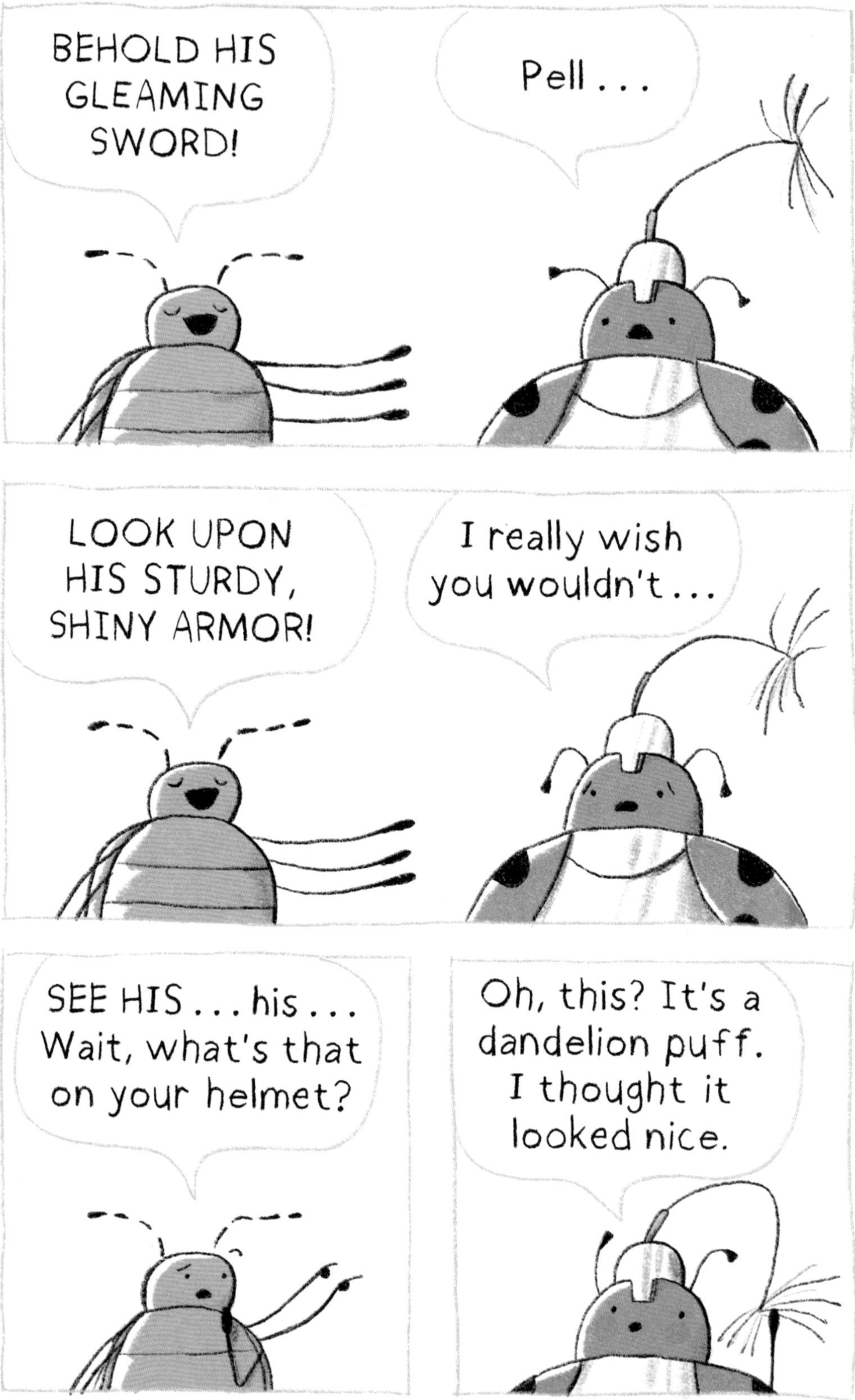
BEHOLD HIS GLEAMING SWORD!
Pell . . .
LOOK UPON HIS STURDY, SHINY ARMOR!
I really wish you wouldn't . . .
SEE HIS . . . his . . . Wait, what's that on your helmet?
Oh, this? It's a dandelion puff. I thought it looked nice.

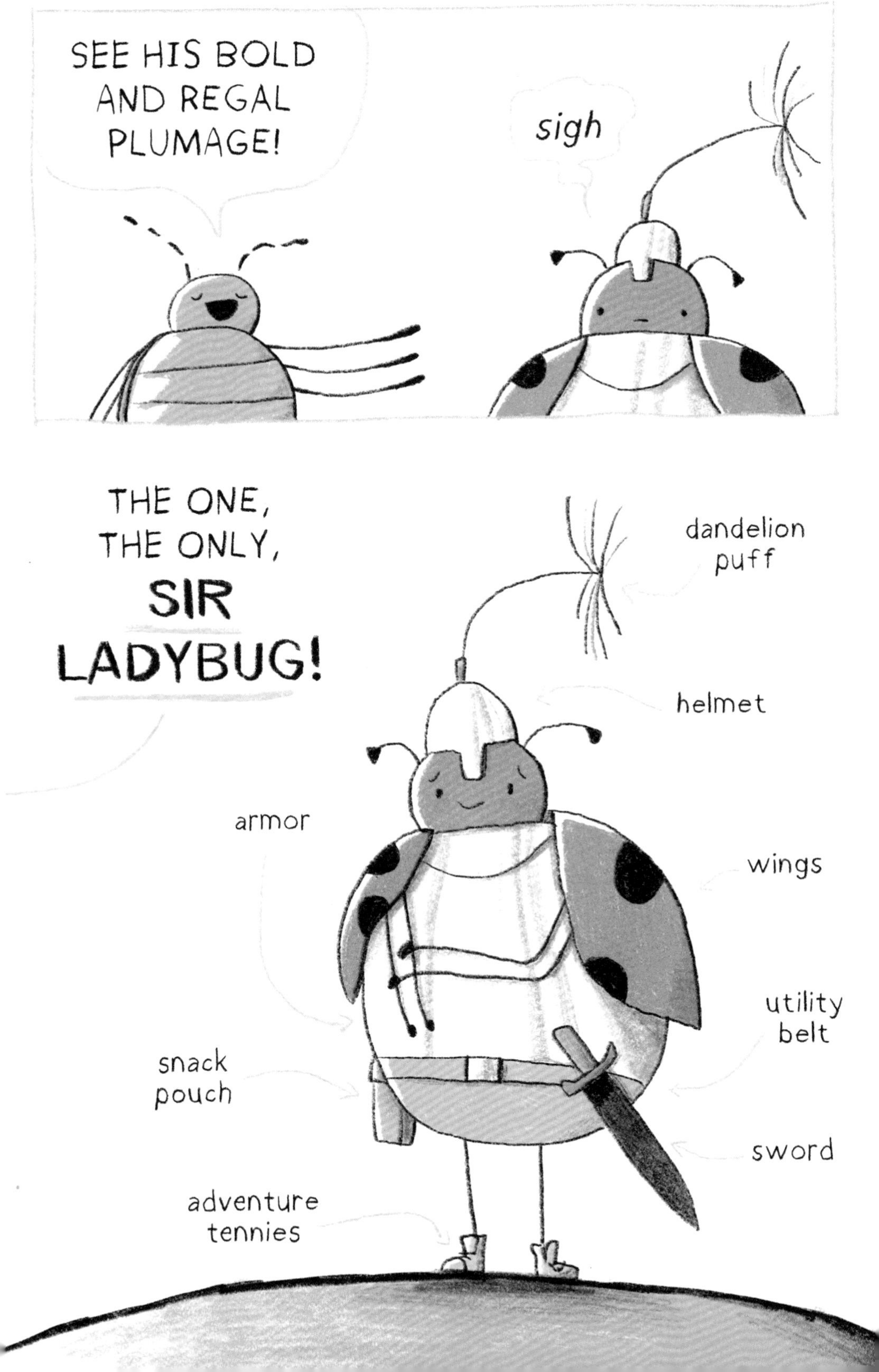

SEE HIS BOLD AND REGAL PLUMAGE!
sigh
THE ONE, THE ONLY, SIR LADYBUG!
dandelion puff
helmet
armor
wings
utility belt
snack pouch
sword
adventure tennies

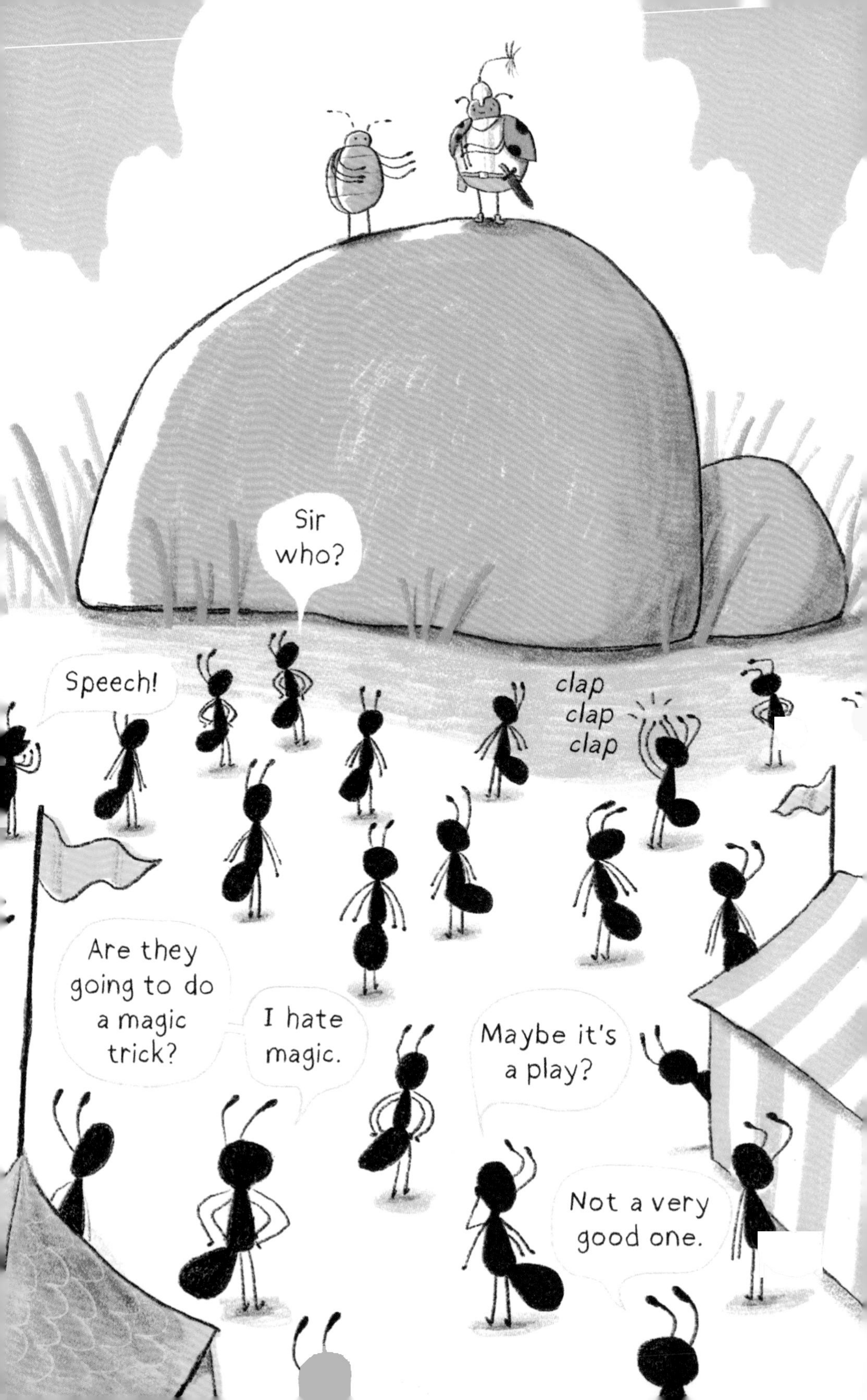
Sir who?
Speech!
clap clap clap
Are they going to do a magic trick?
I hate magic.
Maybe it's a play?
Not a very good one.

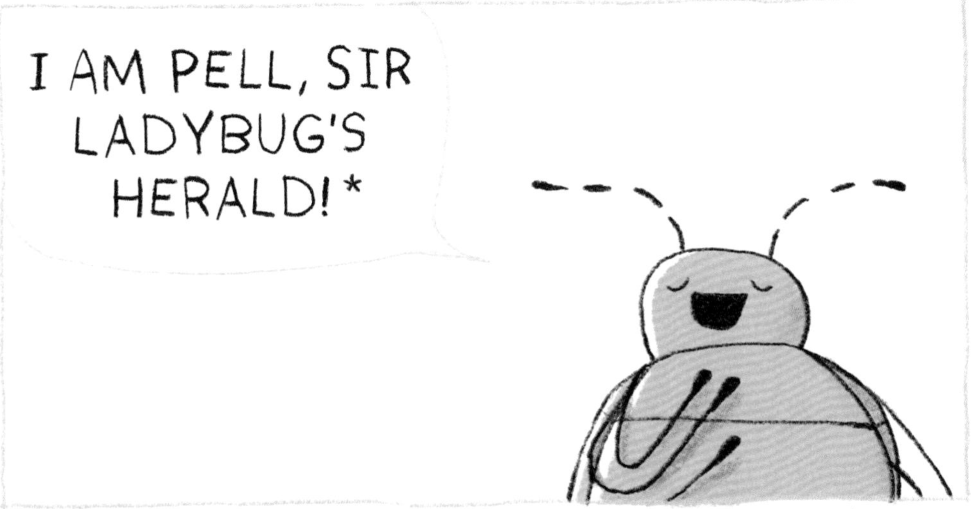
I AM PELL, SIR LADYBUG'S HERALD!*

*__herald__: best friend and bug who hollers about things

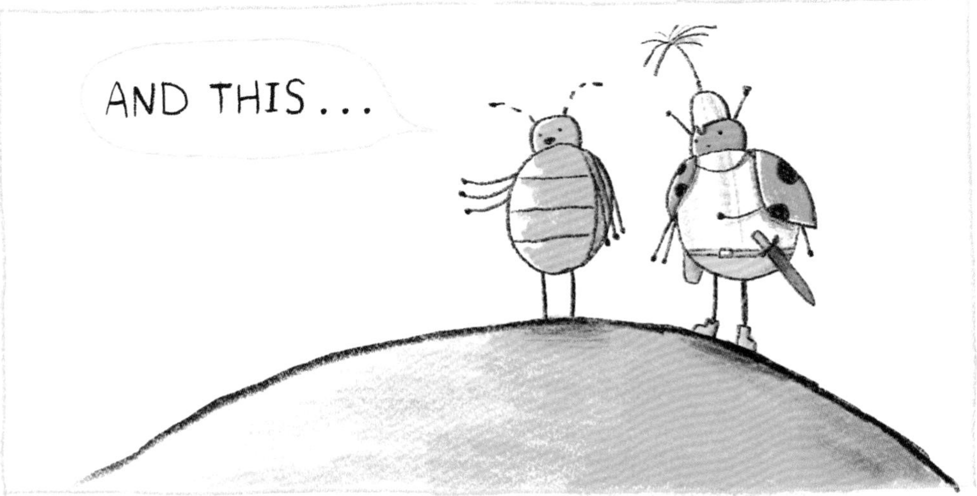
AND THIS . . .

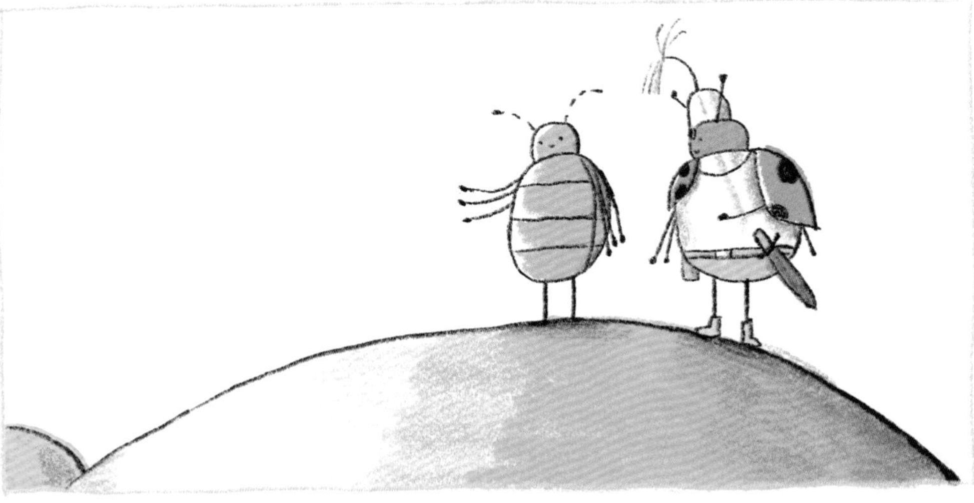

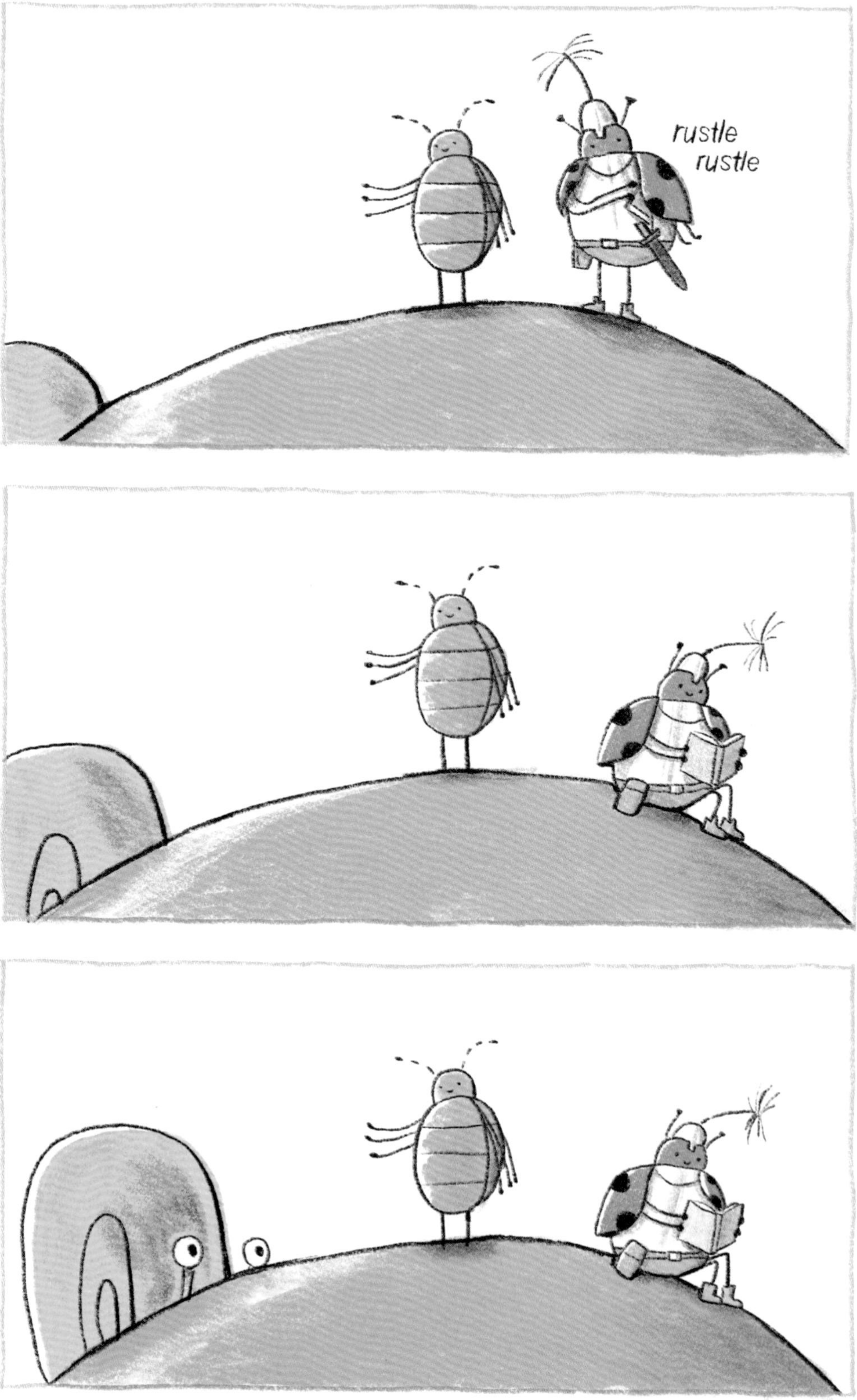
rustle
rustle

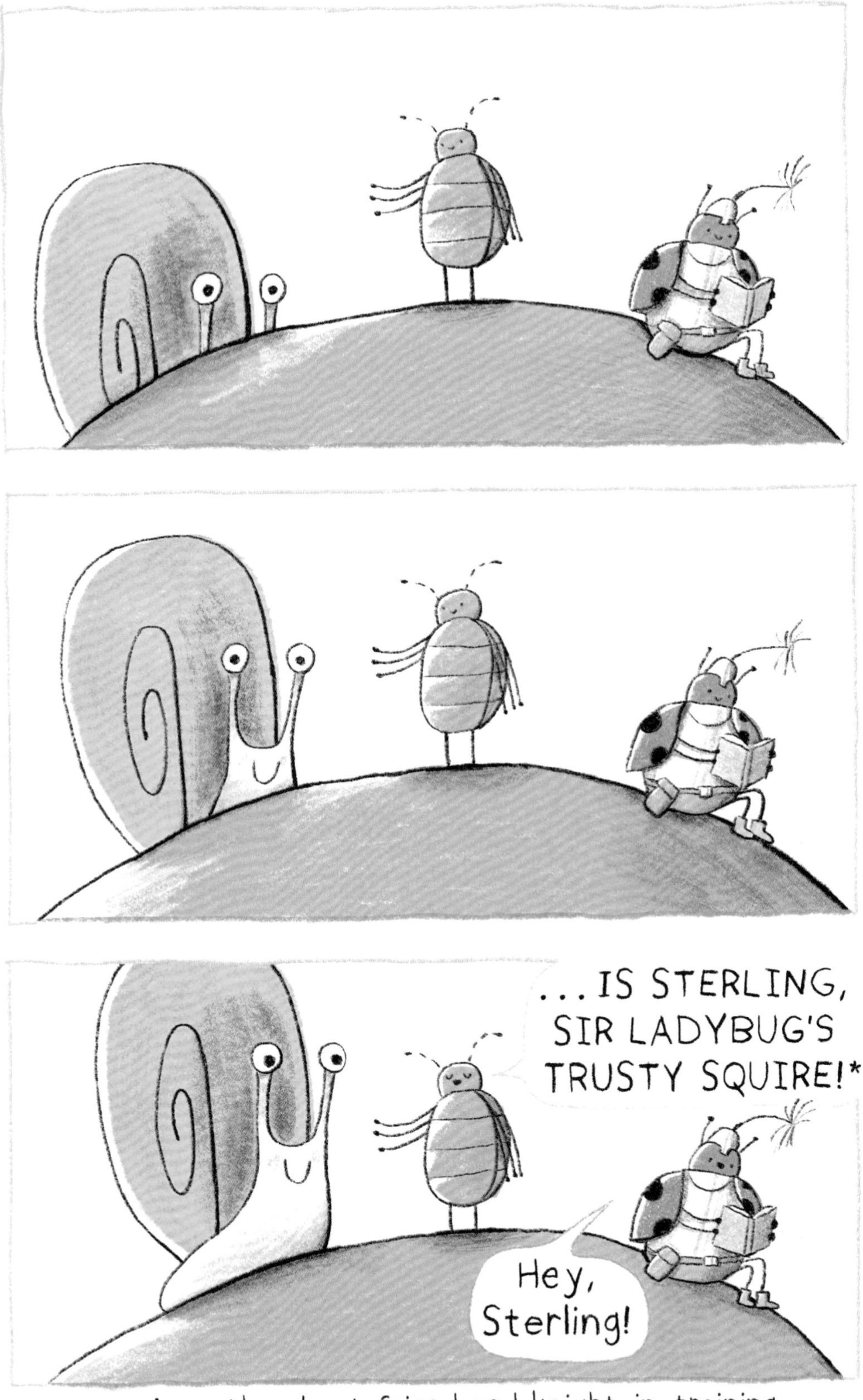
...IS STERLING, SIR LADYBUG'S TRUSTY SQUIRE!*
Hey, Sterling!

***squire**: other best friend and knight-in-training

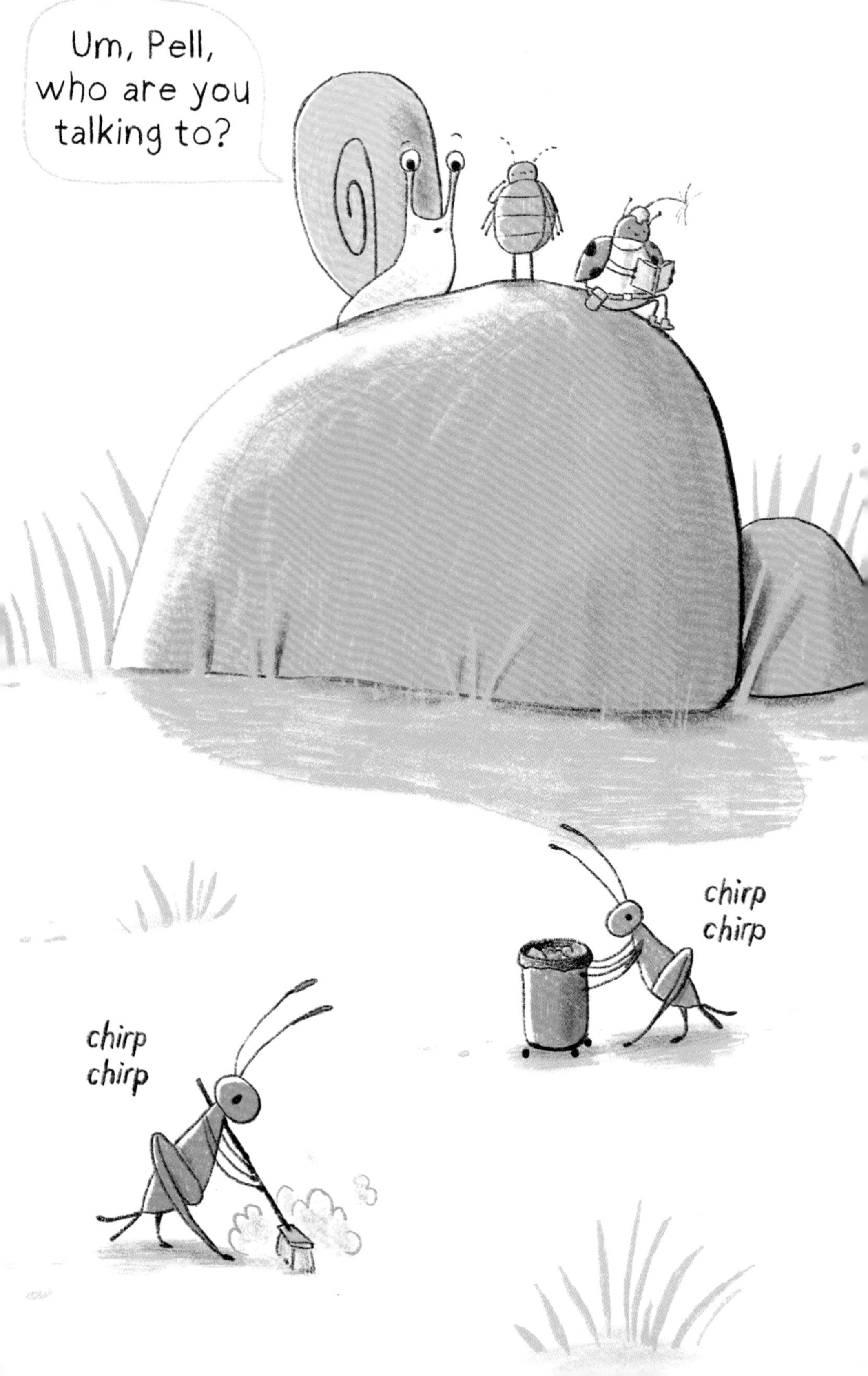
Um, Pell, who are you talking to?
chirp chirp
chirp chirp

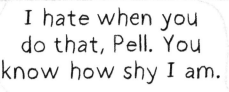

I hate when you do that, Pell. You know how shy I am.

But every knight needs a herald!

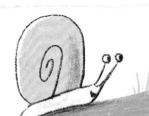

And a trusty squire!

How else will they know how important you are?

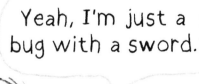

Important? I'm just a bug.

With a **sword!**

Yeah, I'm just a bug with a sword.

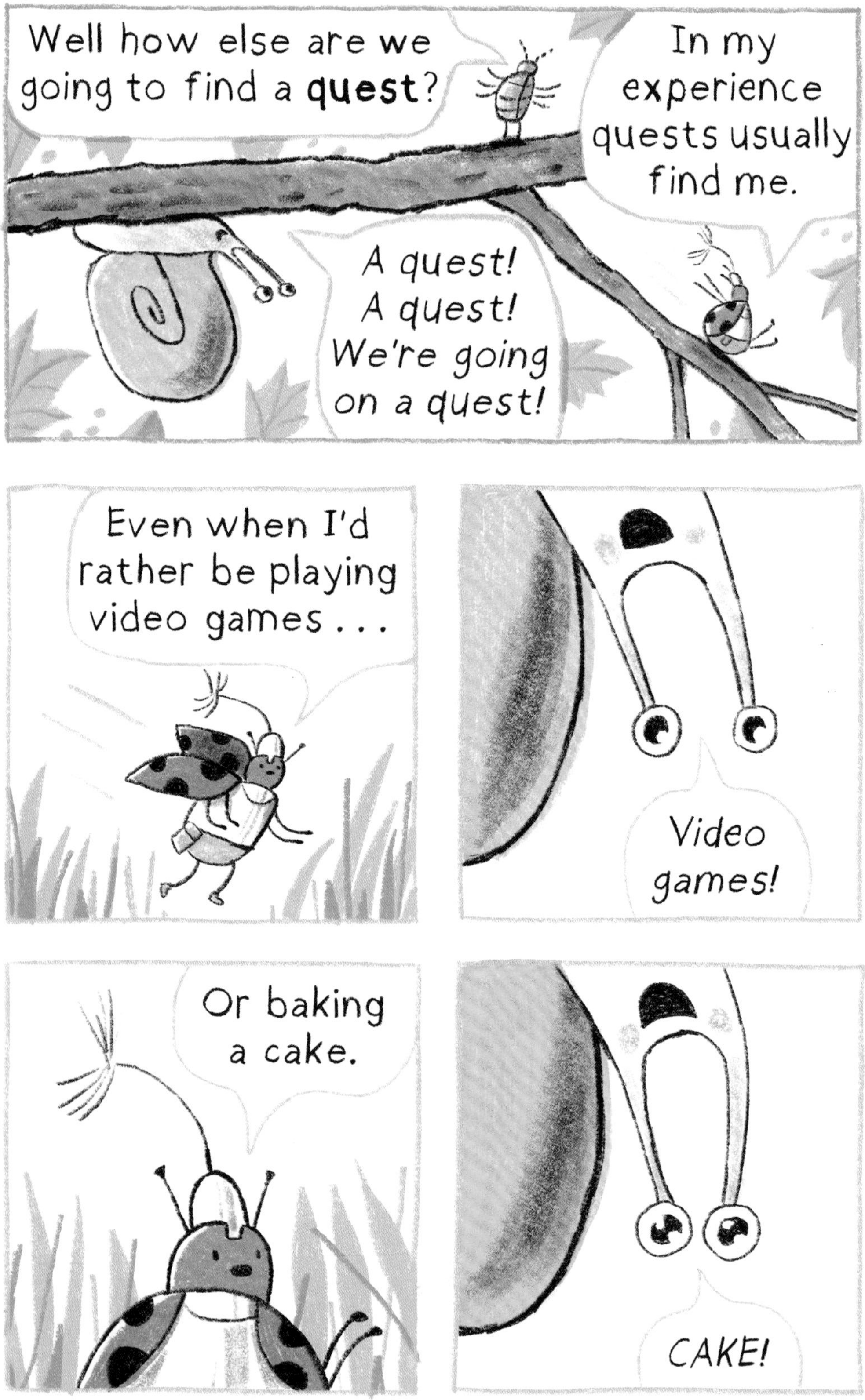
Well how else are we going to find a **quest**?
In my experience quests usually find me.
A quest! A quest! We're going on a quest!
Even when I'd rather be playing video games . . .
Video games!
Or baking a cake.
CAKE!

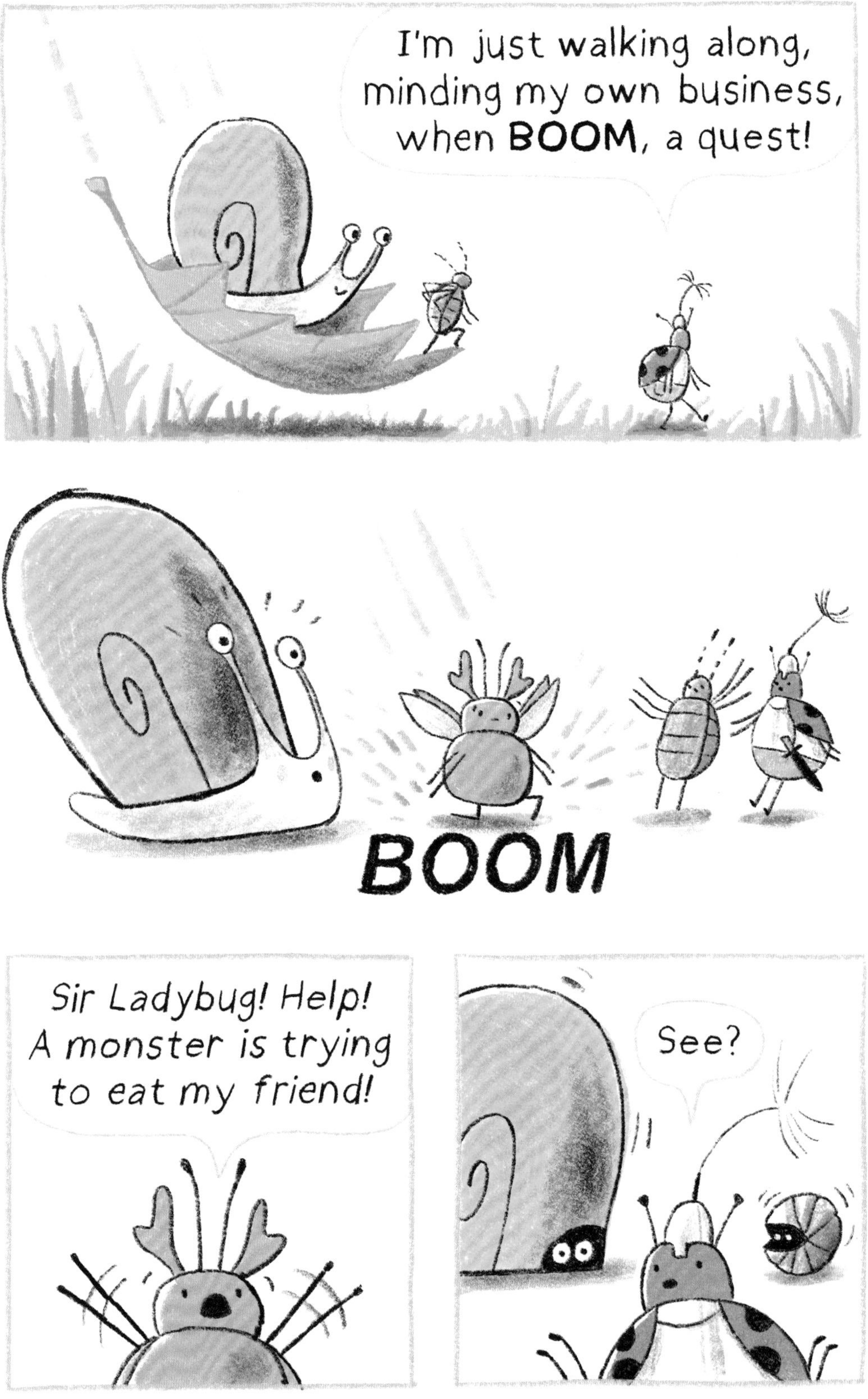
I'm just walking along, minding my own business, when **BOOM**, a quest!
BOOM
Sir Ladybug! Help! A monster is trying to eat my friend!
See?

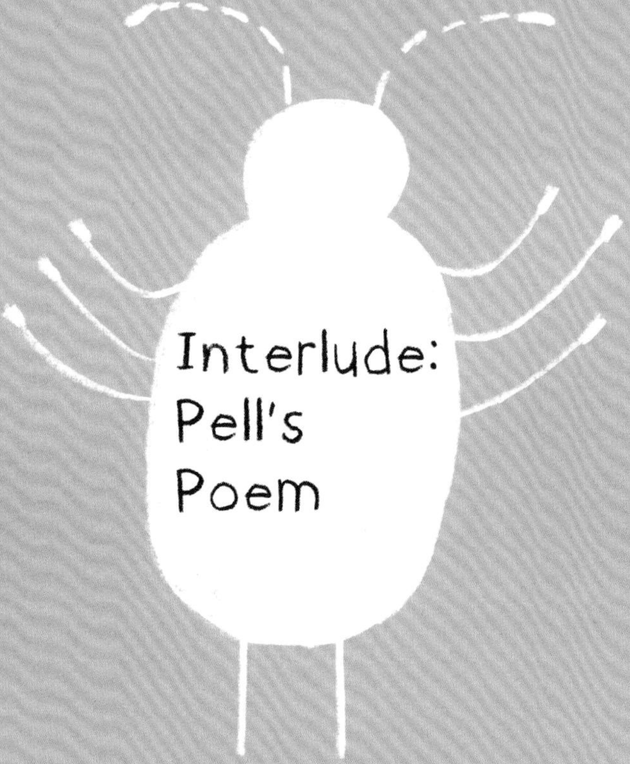

Interlude: Pell's Poem

Sir Ladybug, Sir Ladybug,
the bravest of them all.

He never shirks his duty,
and he'll always take your call.

If you find yourself in danger
call 55 62.

Sir Ladybug will come real quick
and know just what to do.

He slayed a gang of dragon
And squashed some
naughty gnomes.

He waged a war with wizard worms
and chased them from their homes.

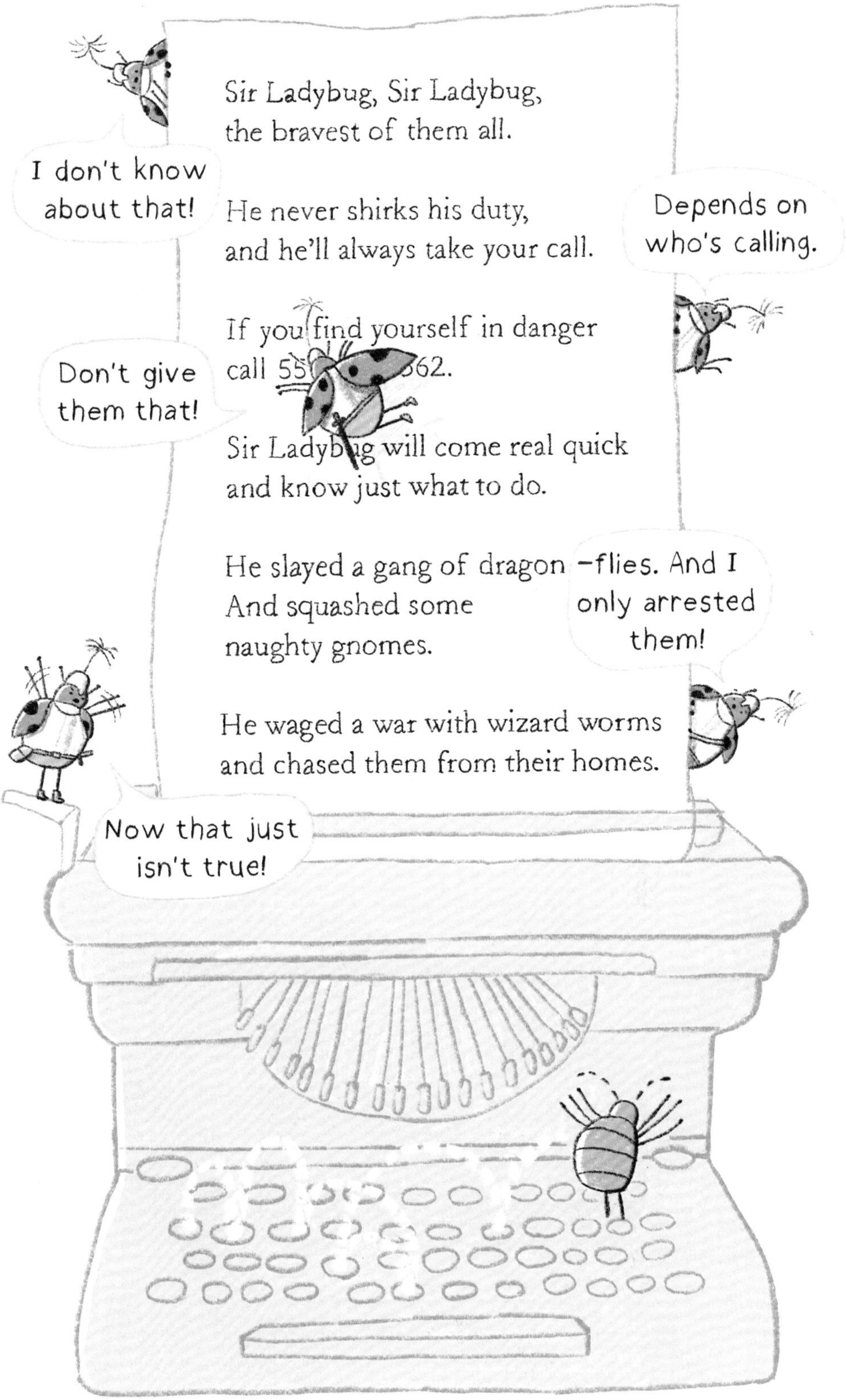
I don't know about that!
Depends on who's calling.
Don't give them that!
-flies. And I only arrested them!
Now that just isn't true!

Chapter 2: The Quest

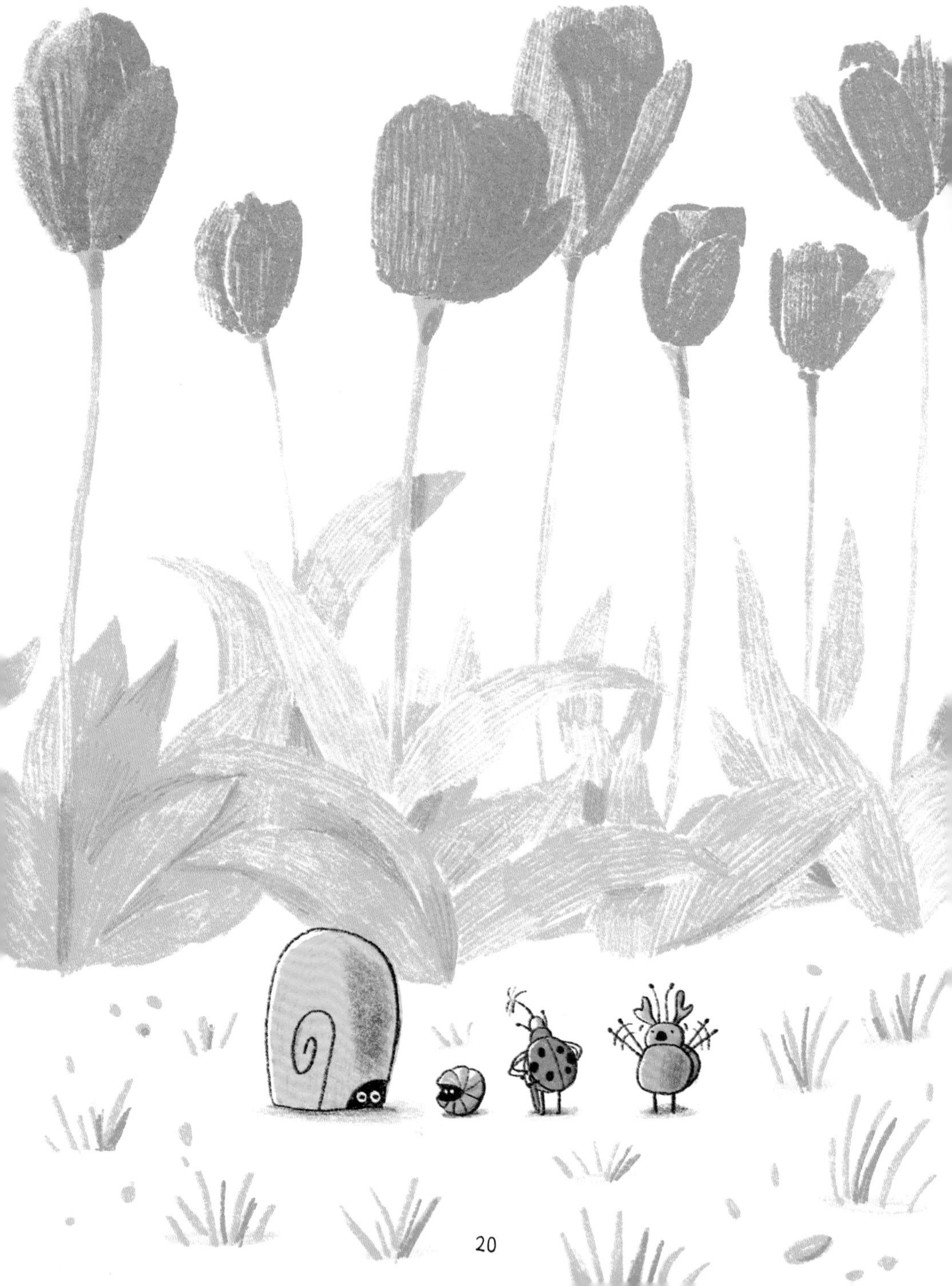

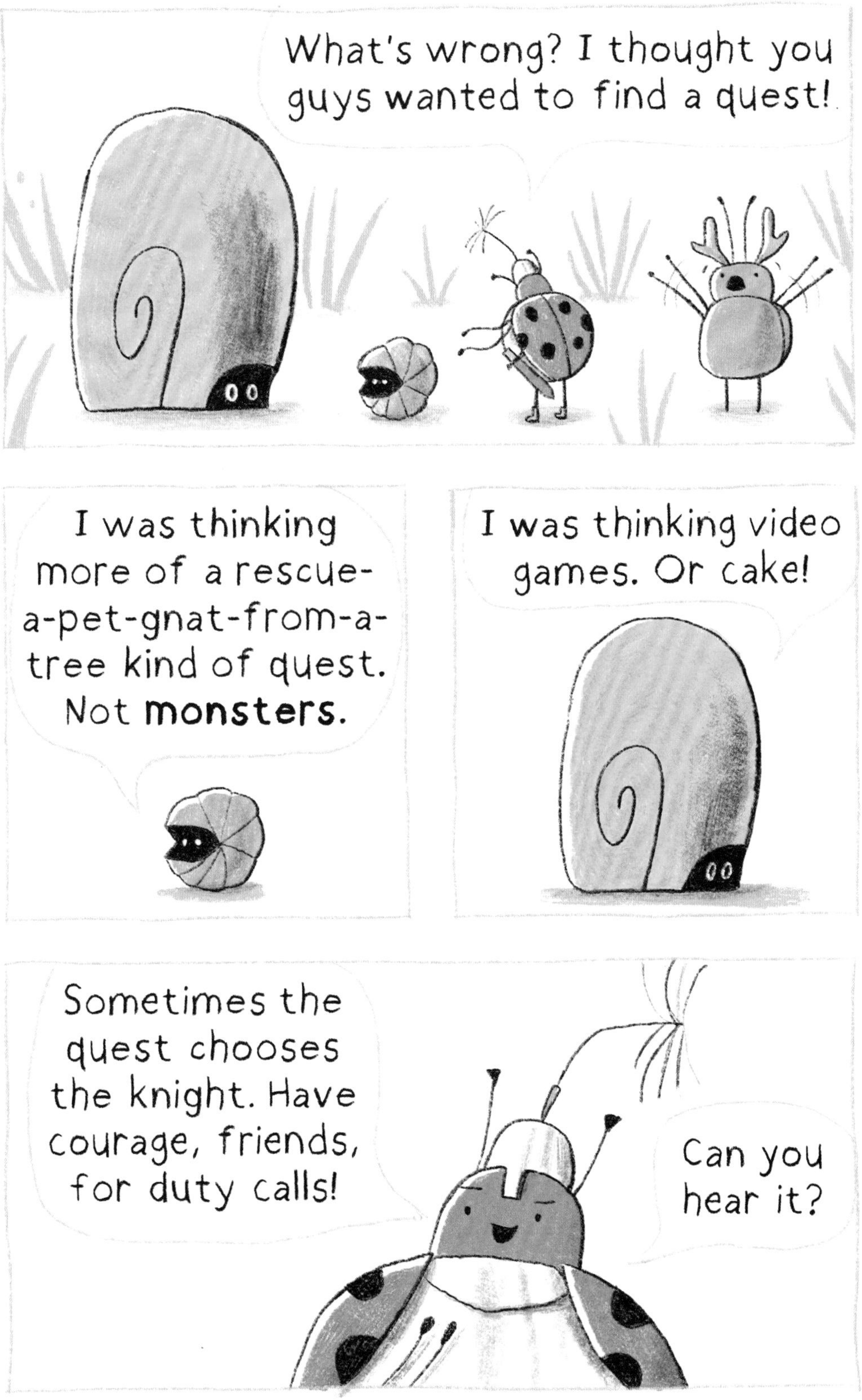
What's wrong? I thought you guys wanted to find a quest!
I was thinking more of a rescue-a-pet-gnat-from-a-tree kind of quest. Not **monsters**.
I was thinking video games. Or cake!
Sometimes the quest chooses the knight. Have courage, friends, for duty calls!
Can you hear it?

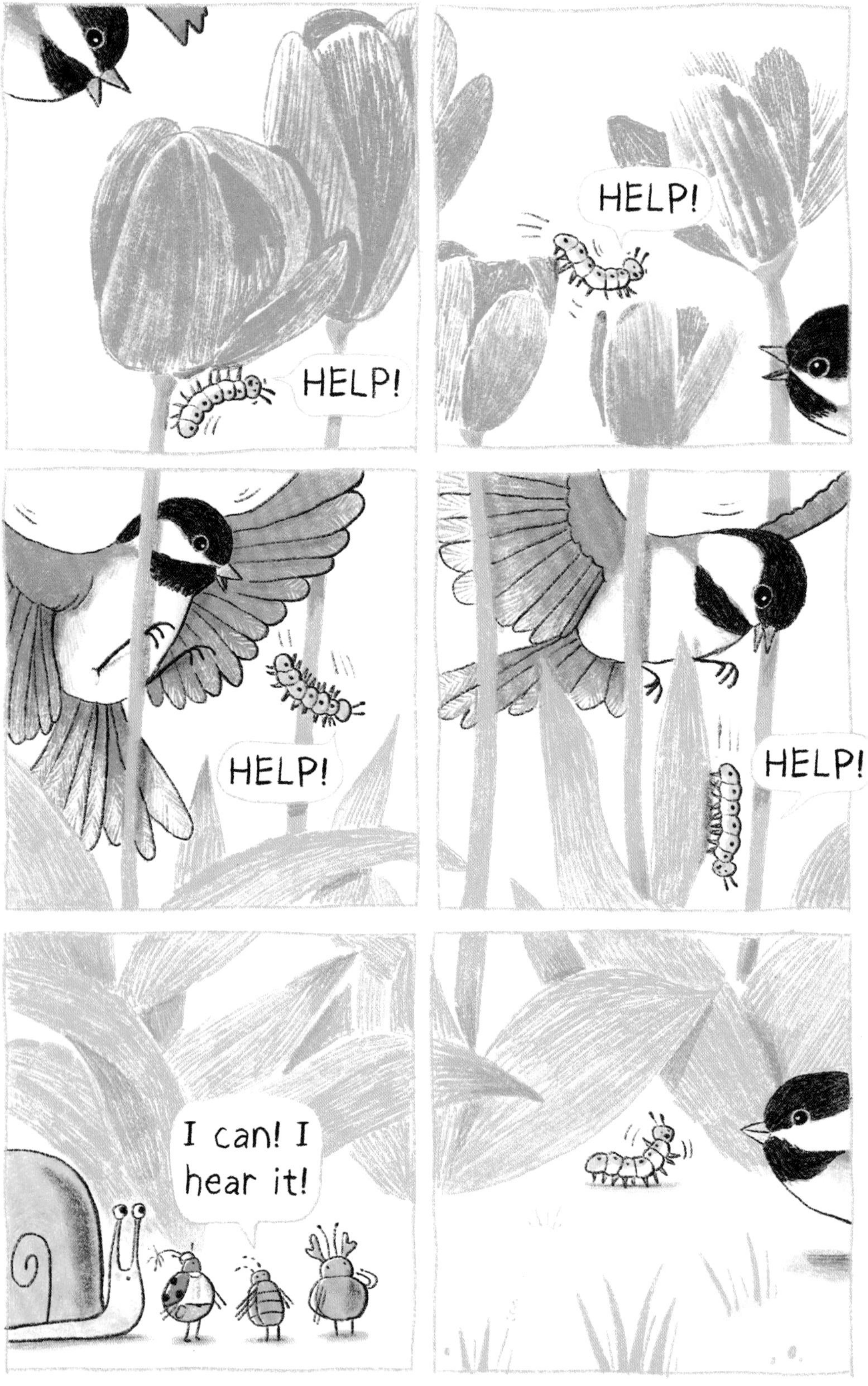
HELP!
HELP!
HELP!
HELP!
I can! I hear it!

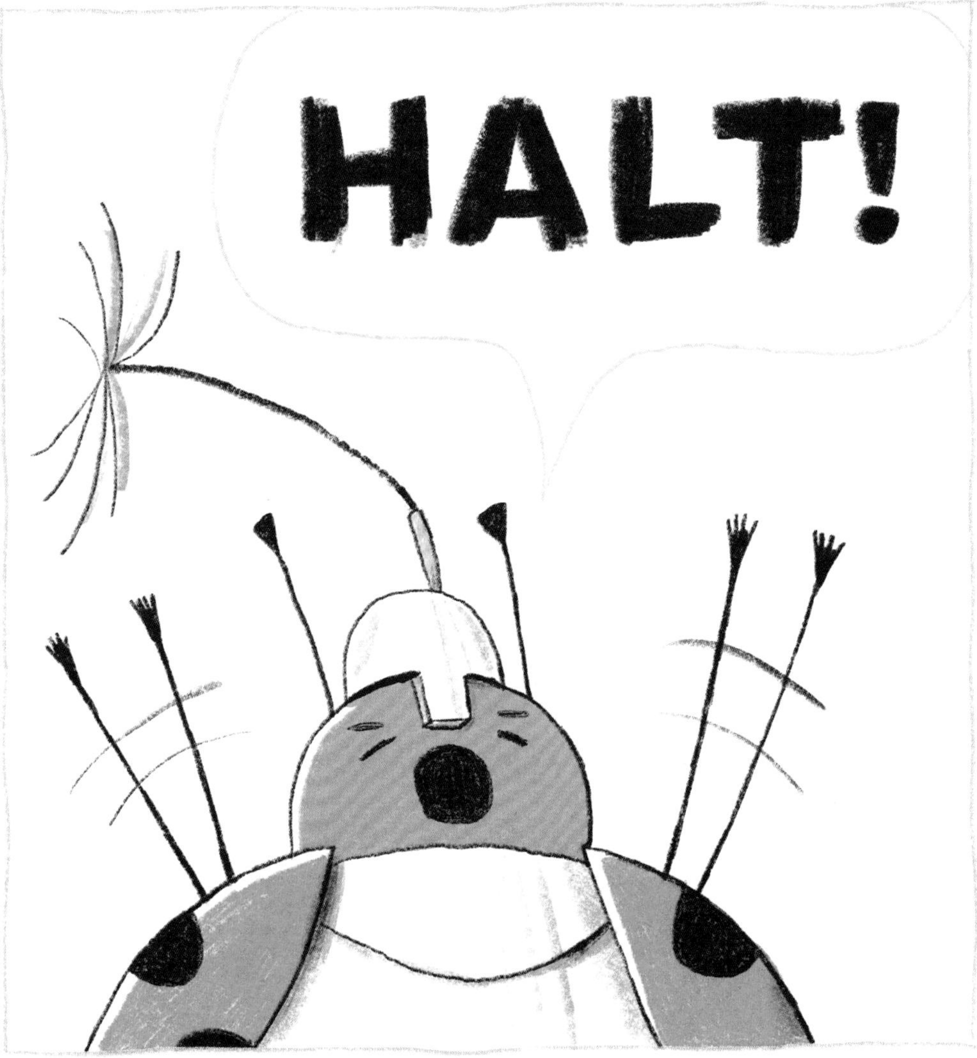
HALT!

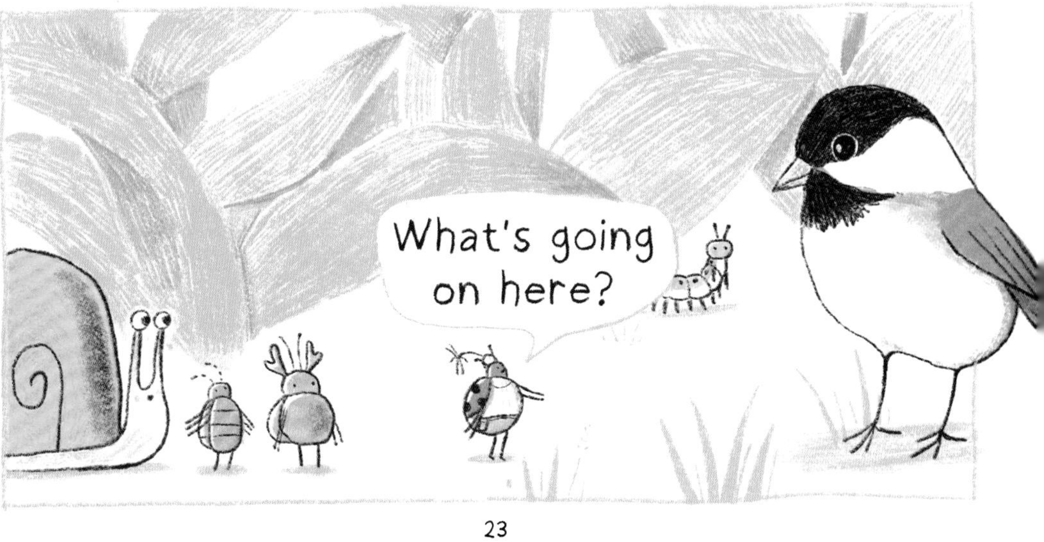
What's going on here?

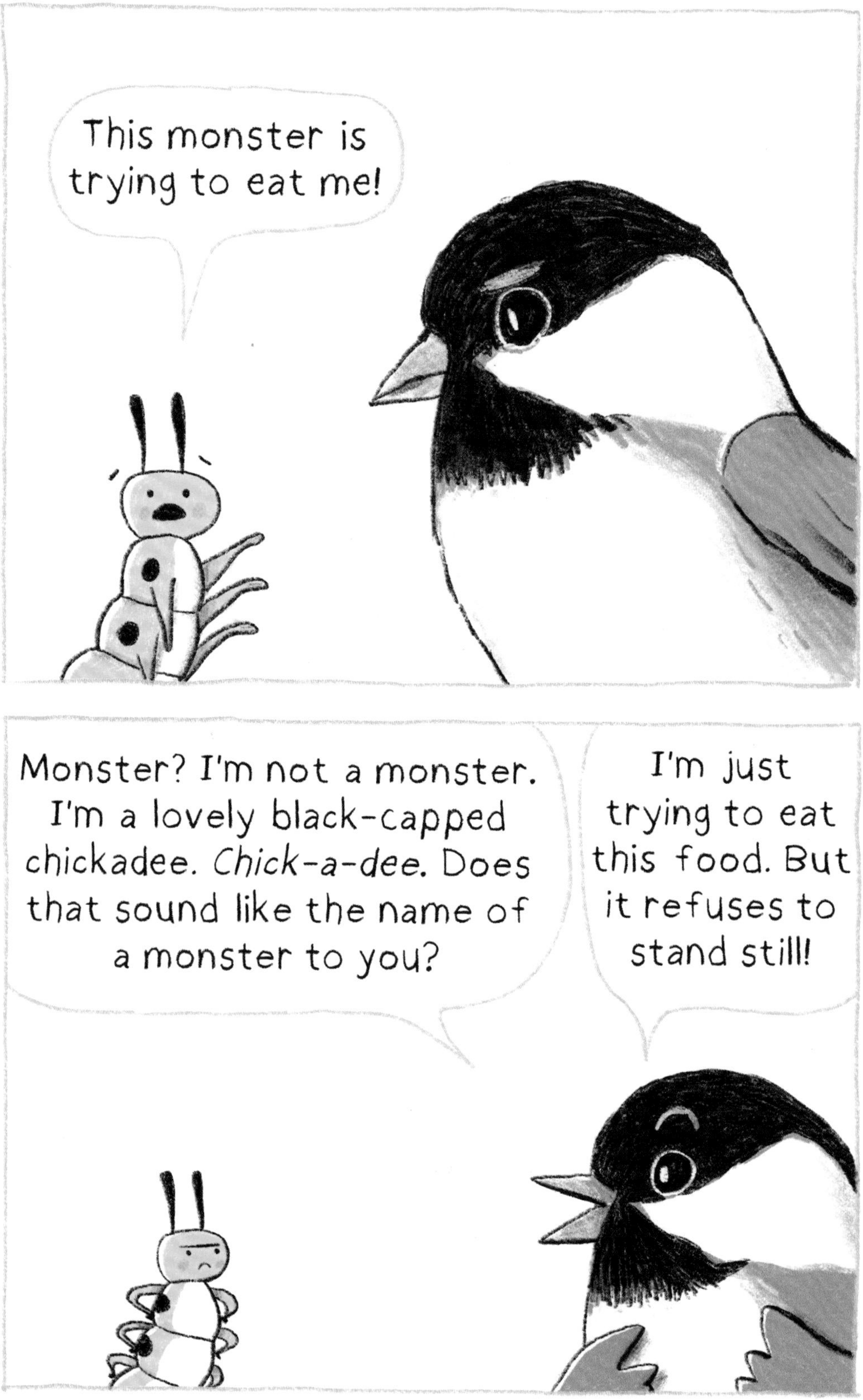
This monster is trying to eat me!
Monster? I'm not a monster. I'm a lovely black-capped chickadee. *Chick-a-dee.* Does that sound like the name of a monster to you?
I'm just trying to eat this food. But it refuses to stand still!

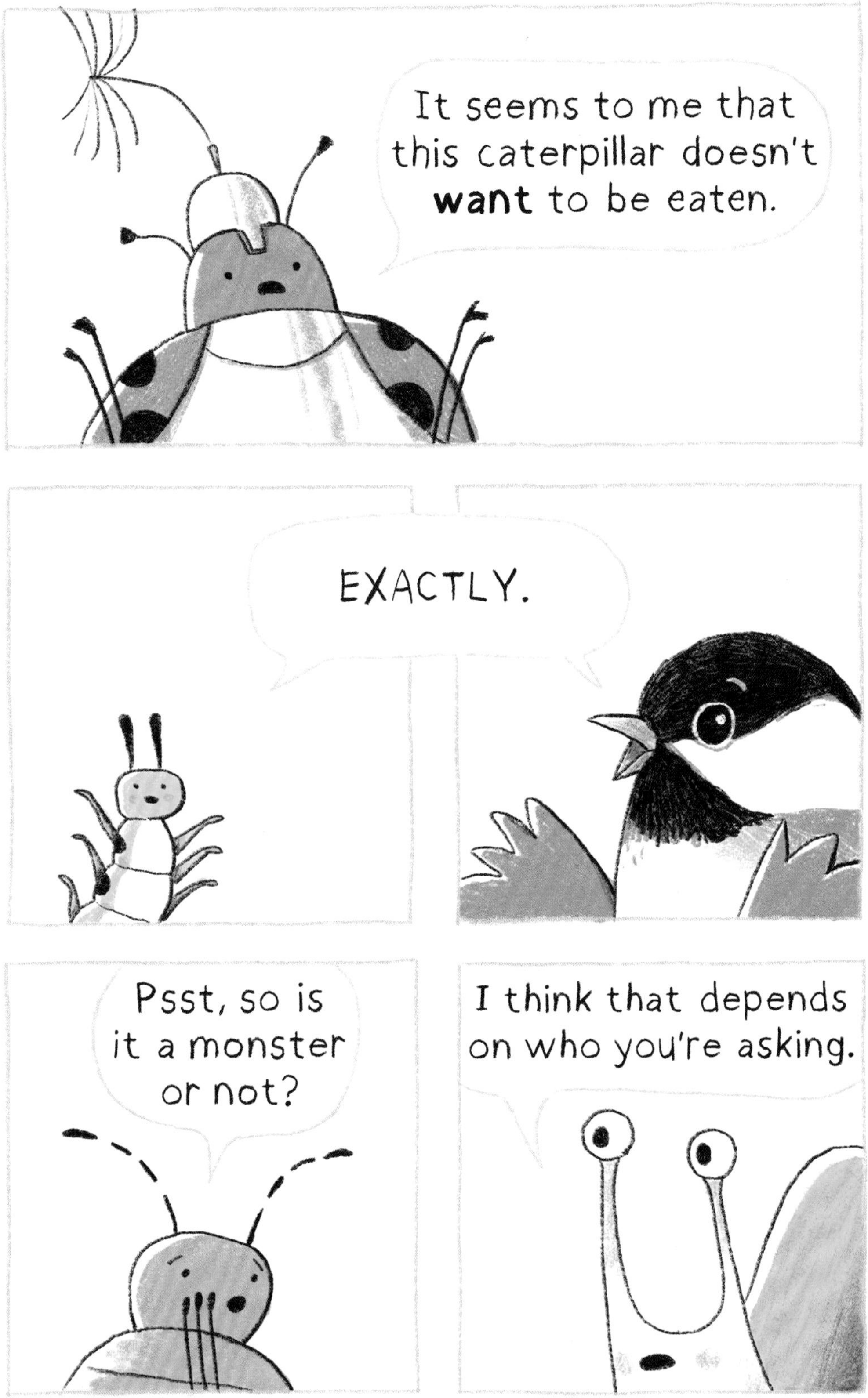
It seems to me that this caterpillar doesn't **want** to be eaten.
EXACTLY.
Psst, so is it a monster or not?
I think that depends on who you're asking.

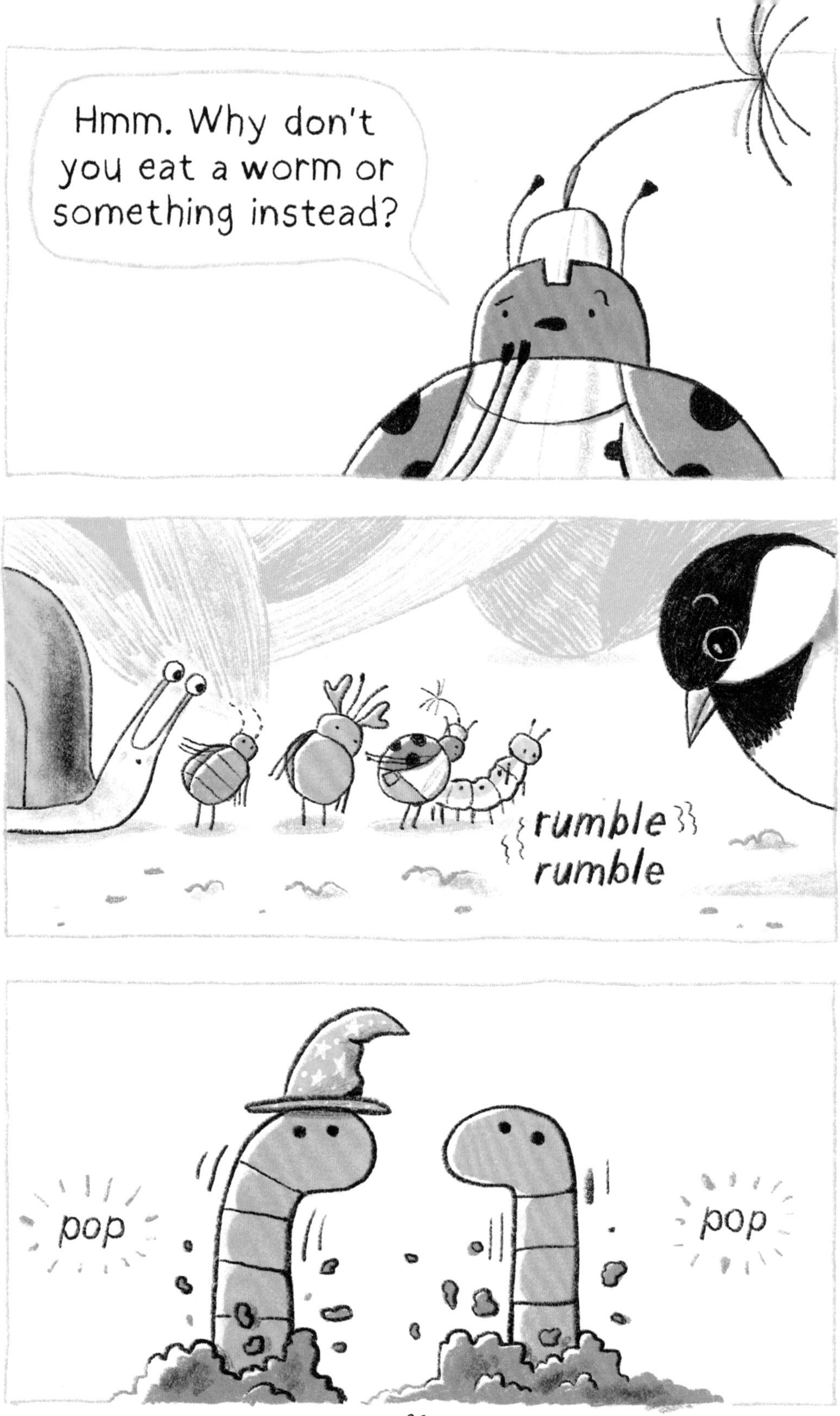
Hmm. Why don't you eat a worm or something instead?
rumble
rumble
pop
pop

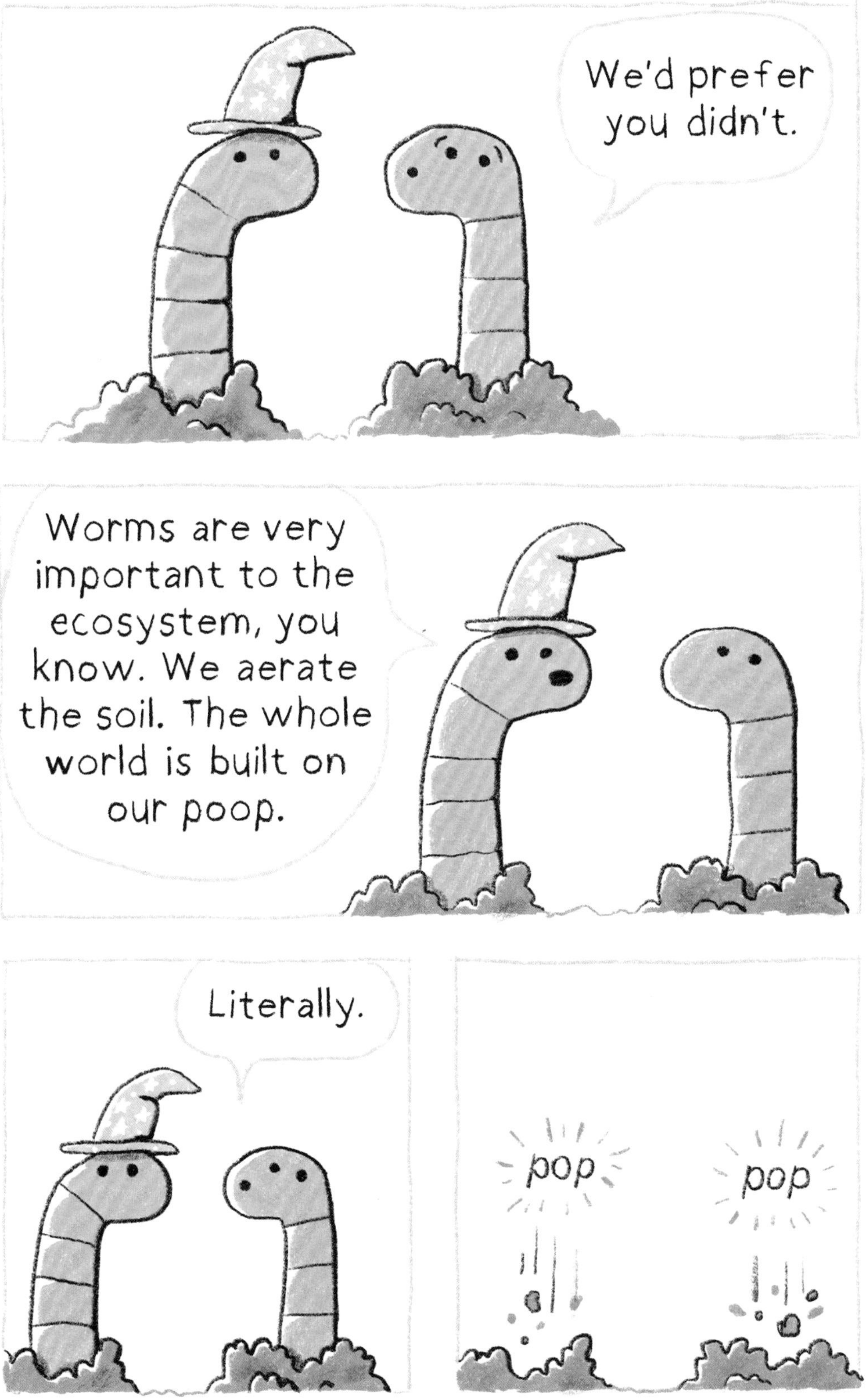
We'd prefer you didn't.
Worms are very important to the ecosystem, you know. We aerate the soil. The whole world is built on our poop.
Literally.
pop
pop

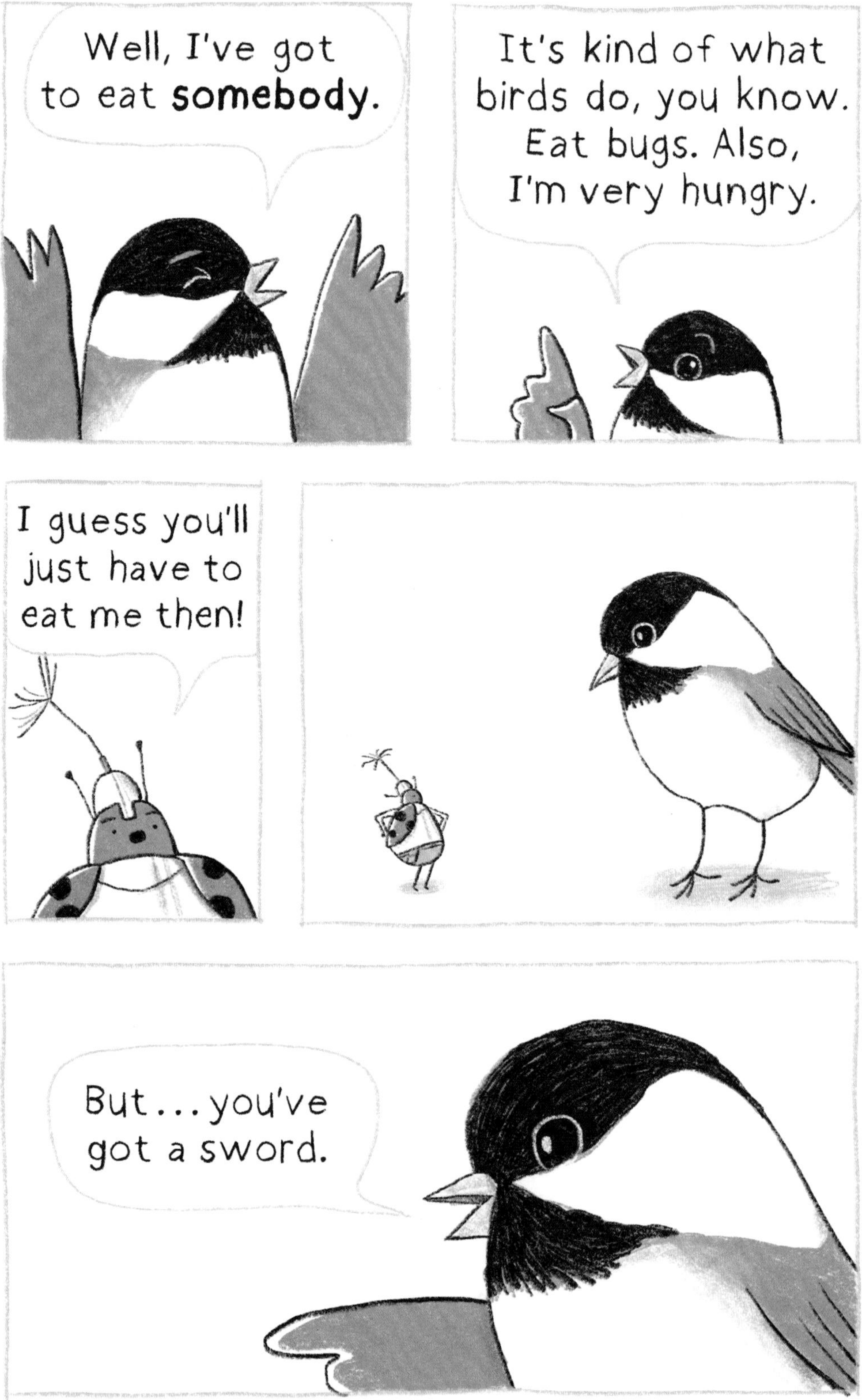
Well, I've got to eat **somebody**.
It's kind of what birds do, you know. Eat bugs. Also, I'm very hungry.
I guess you'll just have to eat me then!
But... you've got a sword.

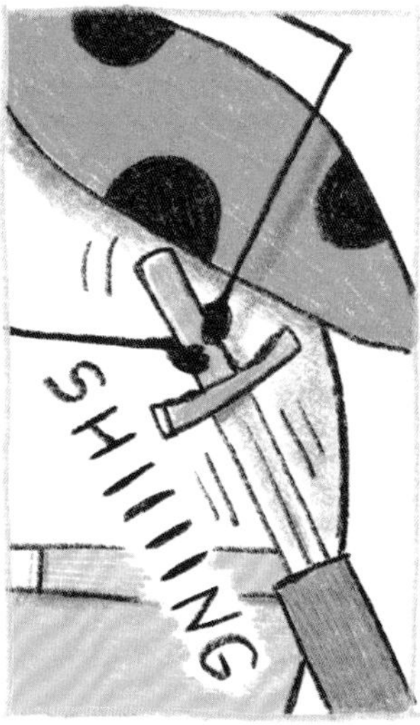
SHIIIING

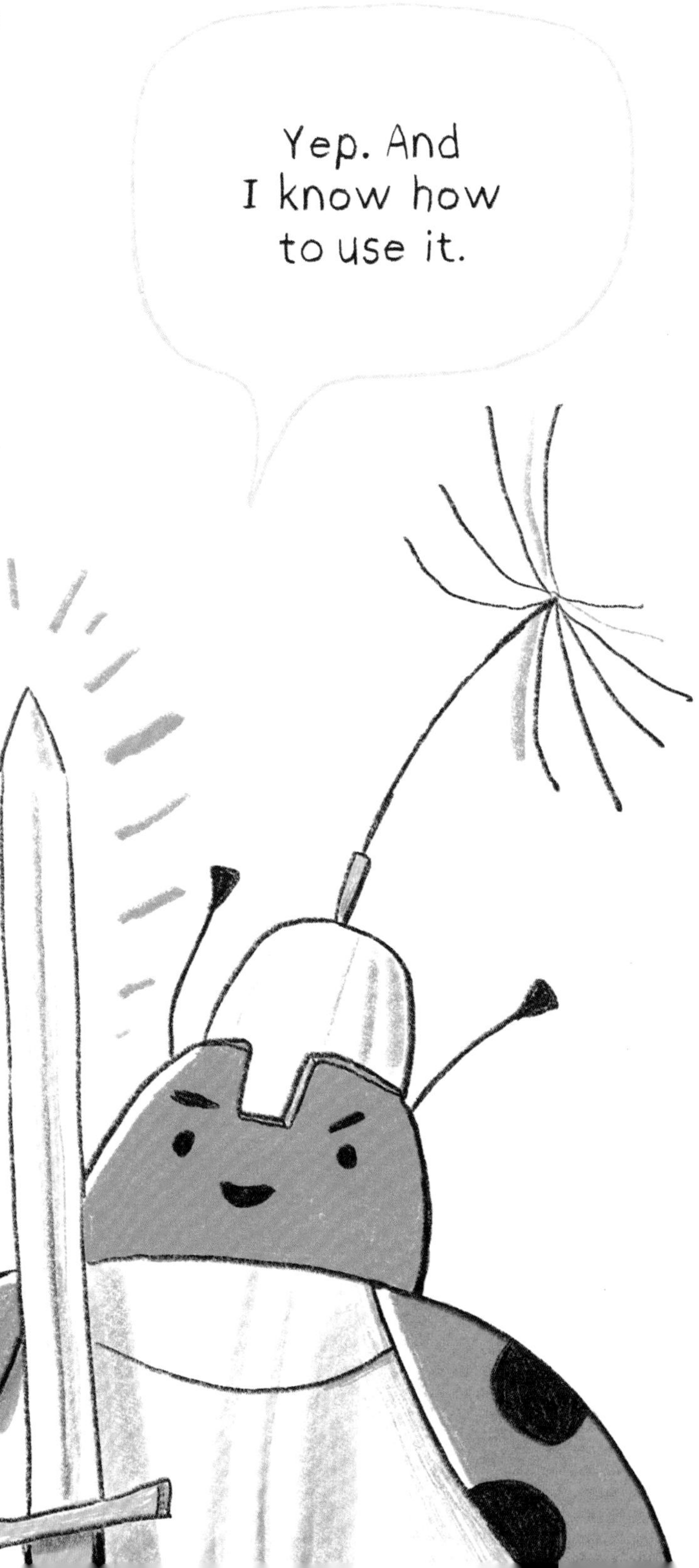
Yep. And
I know how
to use it.

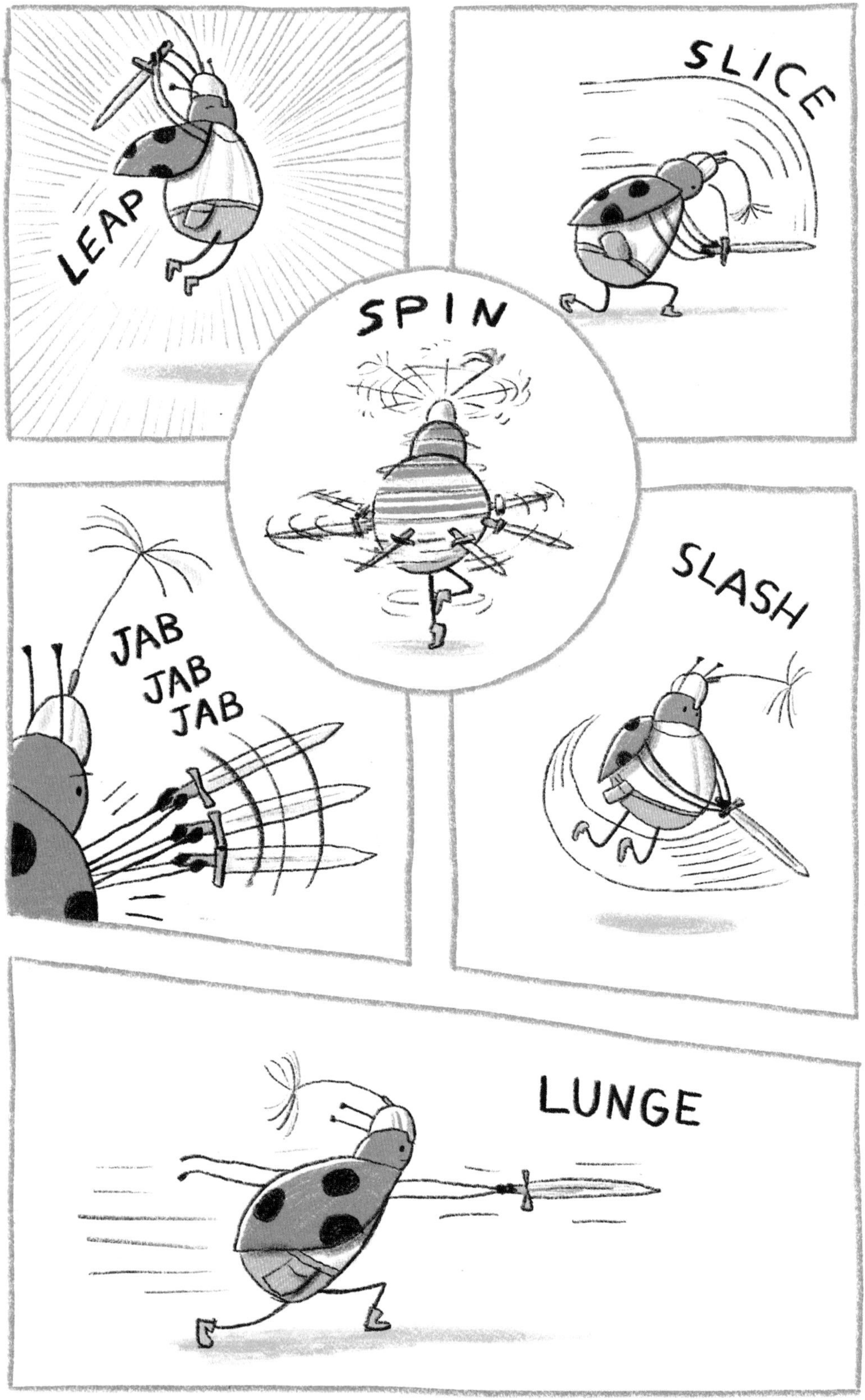
LEAP
SLICE
SPIN
JAB
JAB
JAB
SLASH
LUNGE

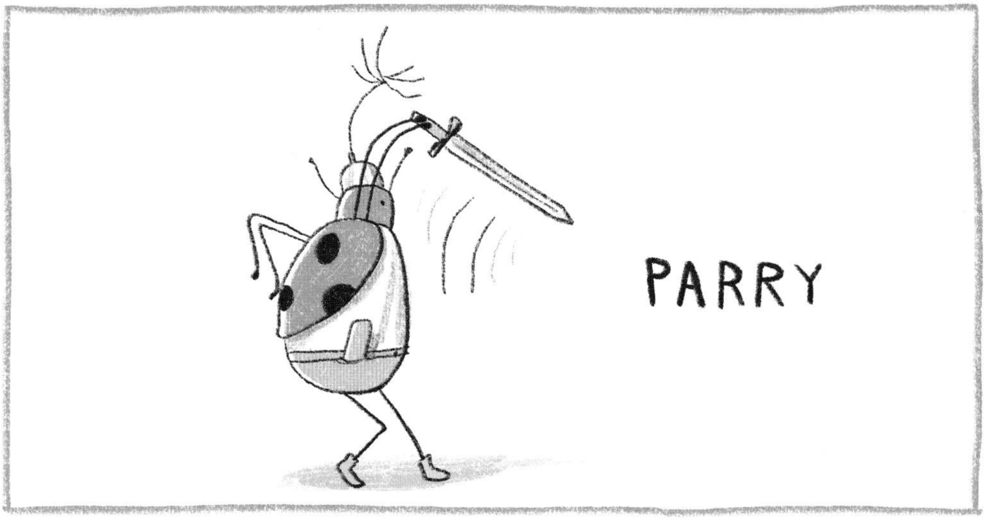
PARRY

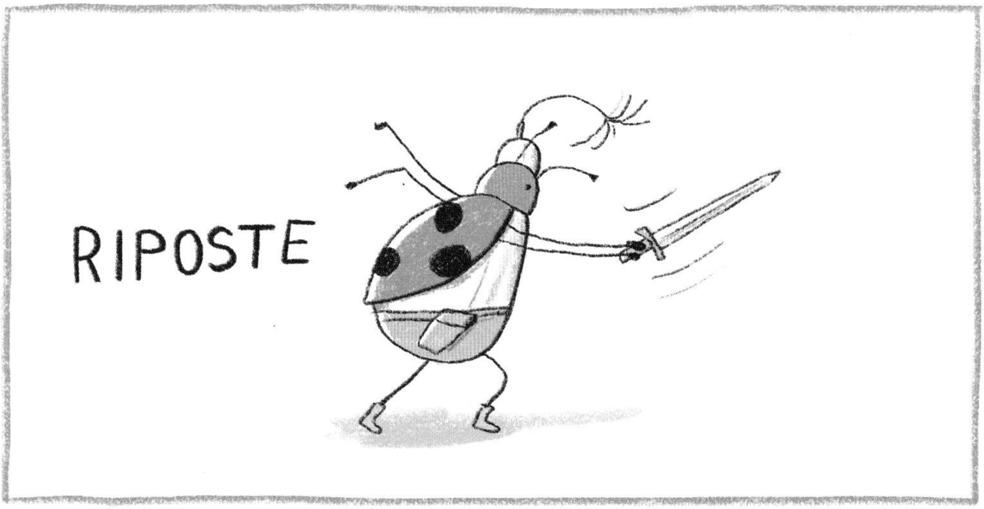
RIPOSTE

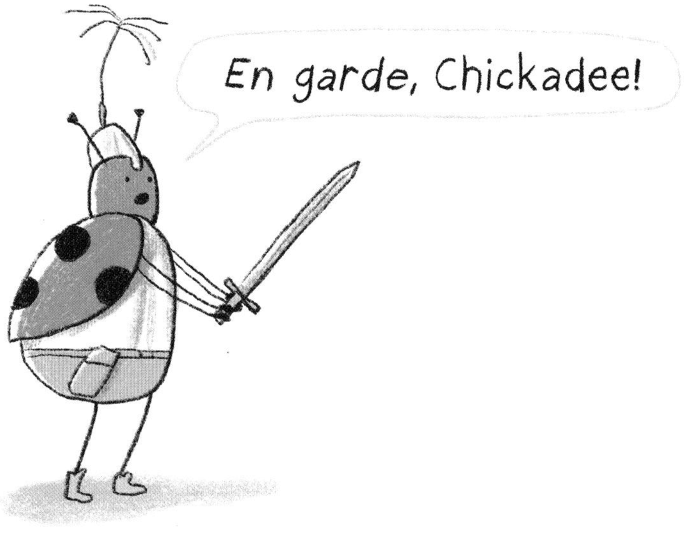
En garde, Chickadee!

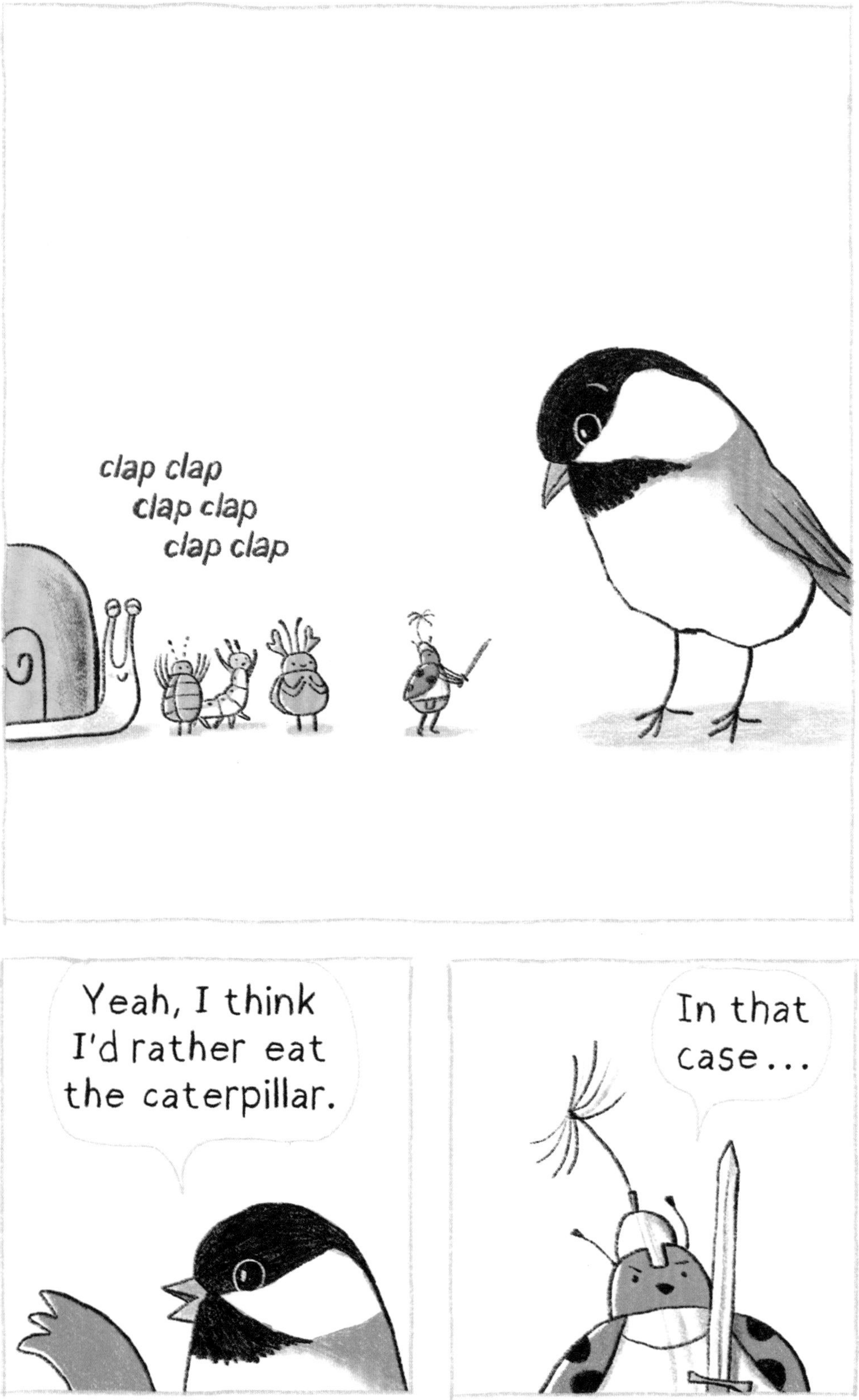
clap clap
clap clap
clap clap
Yeah, I think I'd rather eat the caterpillar.
In that case...

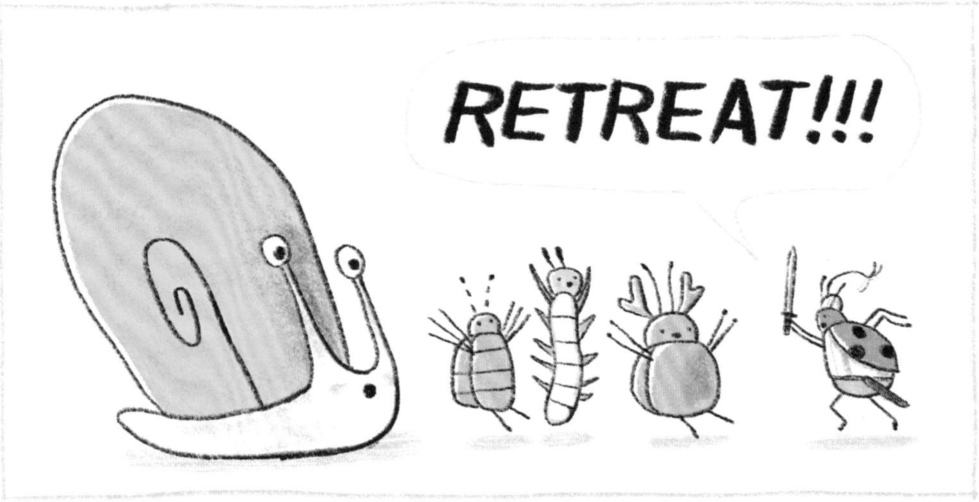
RETREAT!!!

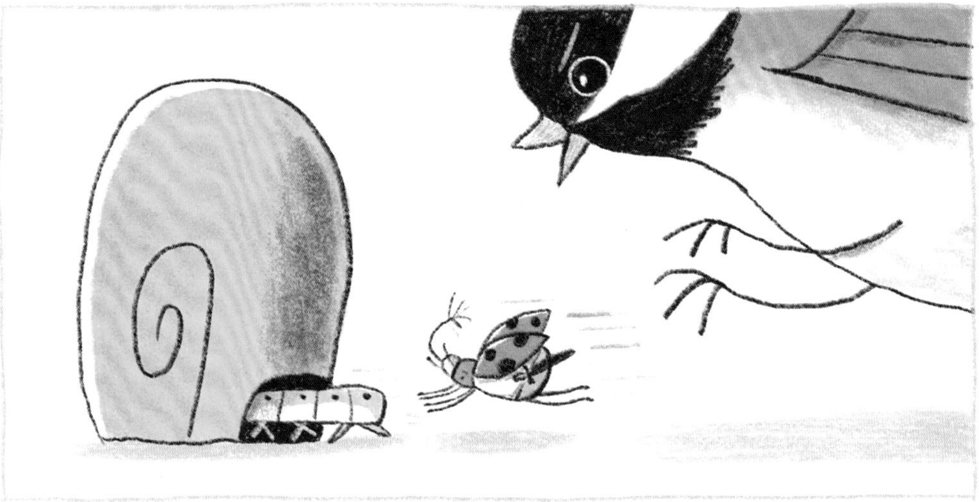

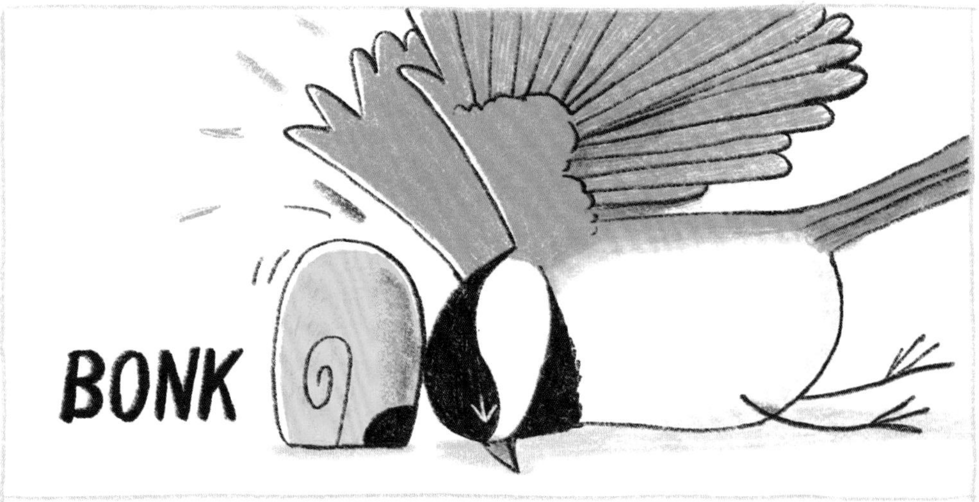
BONK

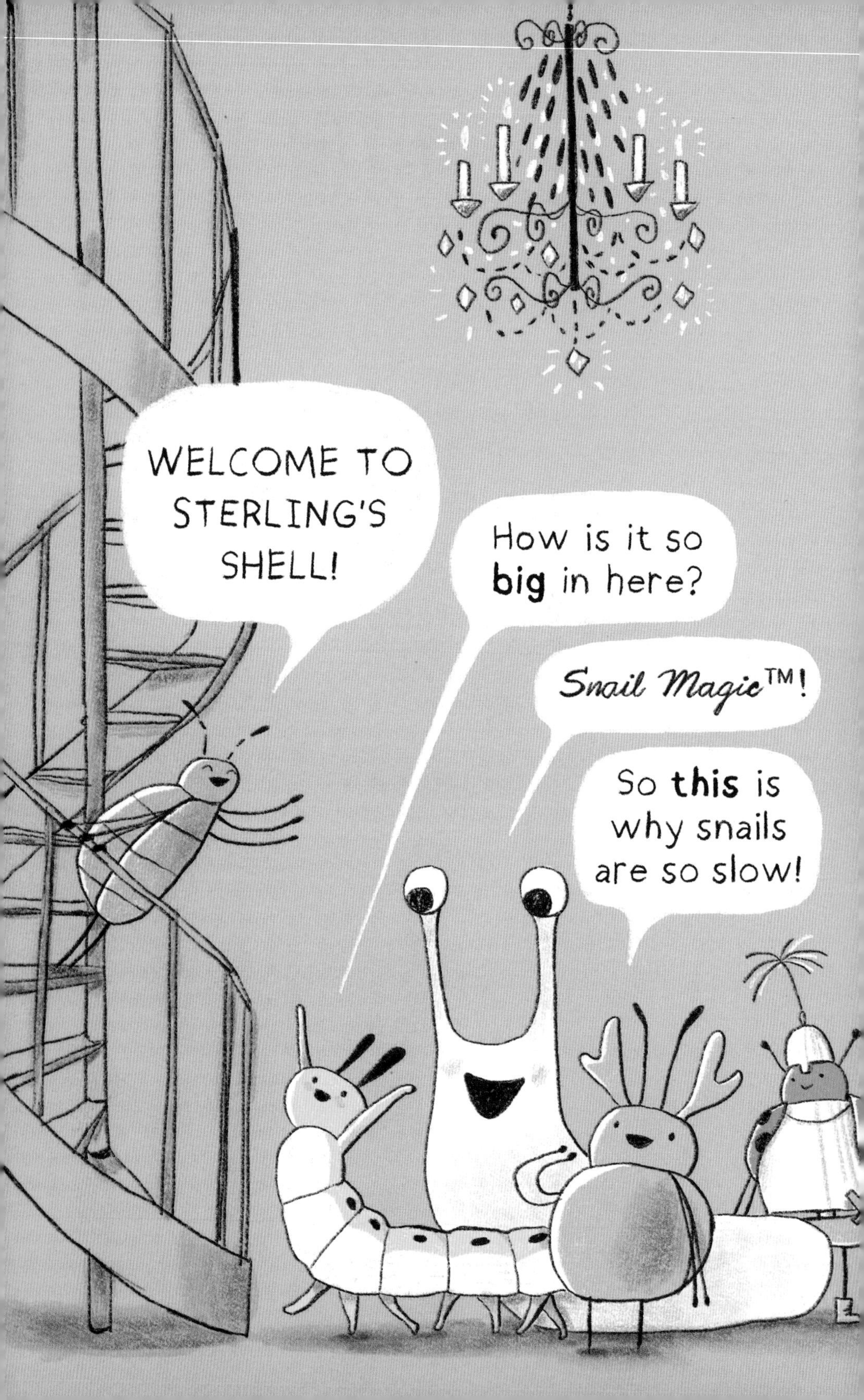
WELCOME TO STERLING'S SHELL!
How is it so **big** in here?
Snail Magic™!
So **this** is why snails are so slow!

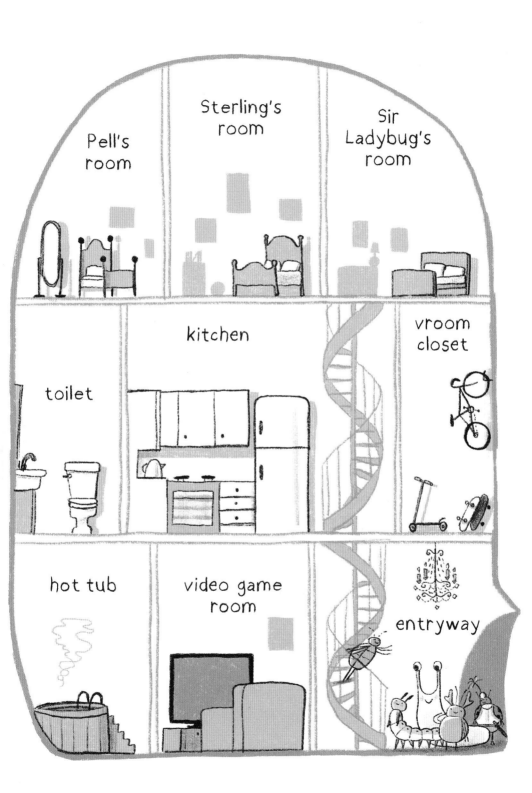

Pell's room

Sterling's room

Sir Ladybug's room

toilet

kitchen

vroom closet

hot tub

video game room

entryway

Chapter 3:
The Plan

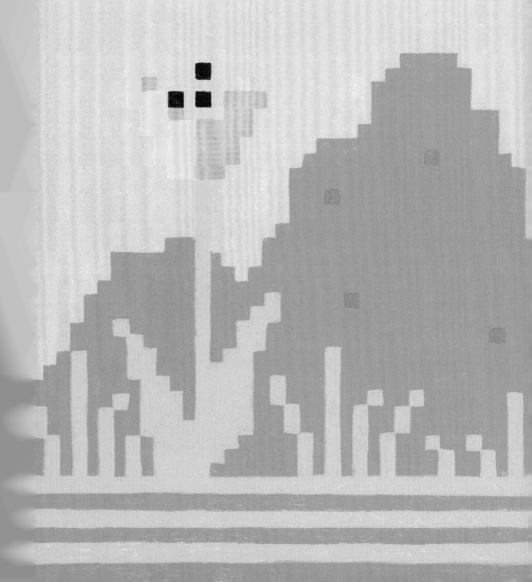

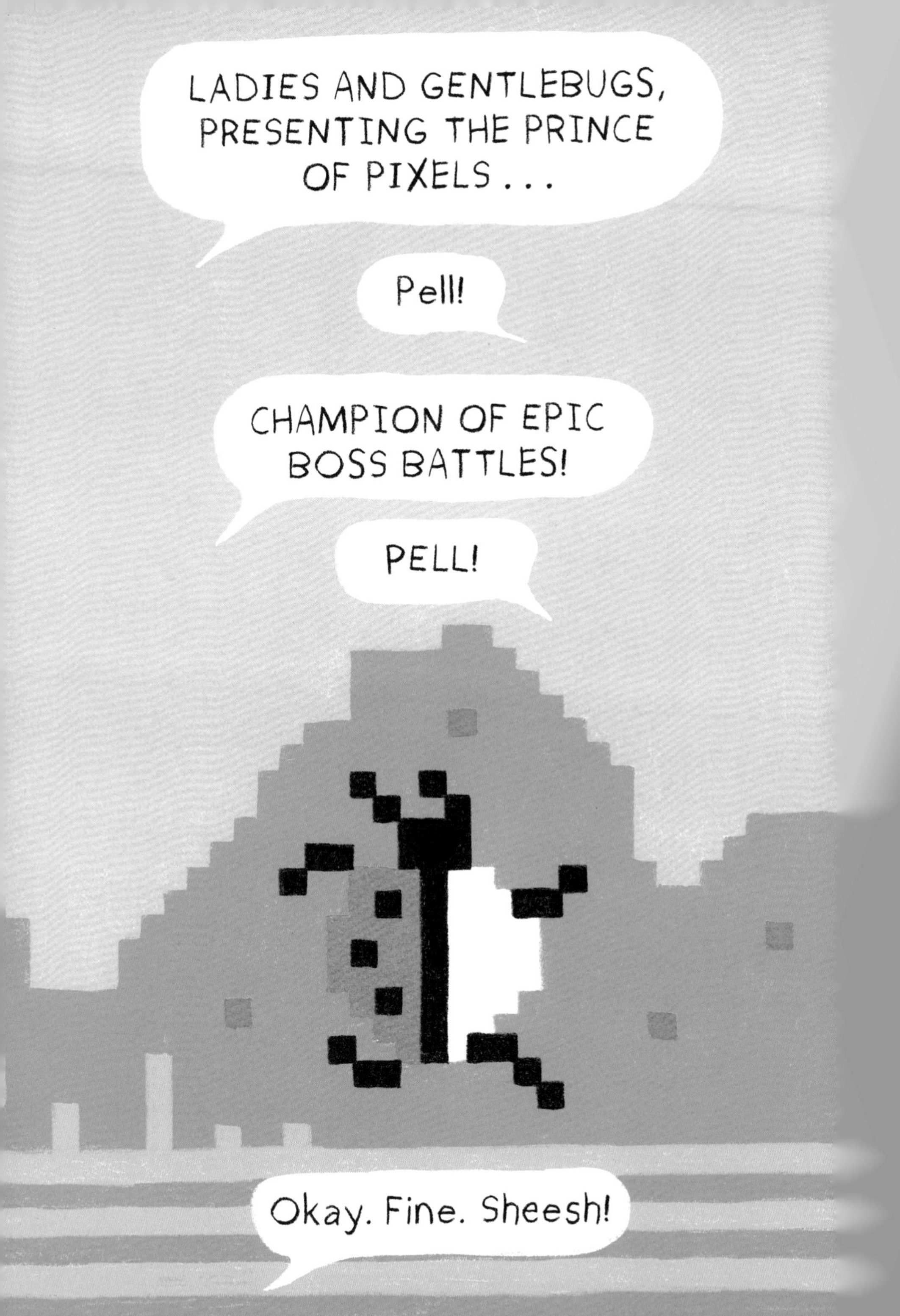
LADIES AND GENTLEBUGS, PRESENTING THE PRINCE OF PIXELS . . .
Pell!
CHAMPION OF EPIC BOSS BATTLES!
PELL!
Okay. Fine. Sheesh!

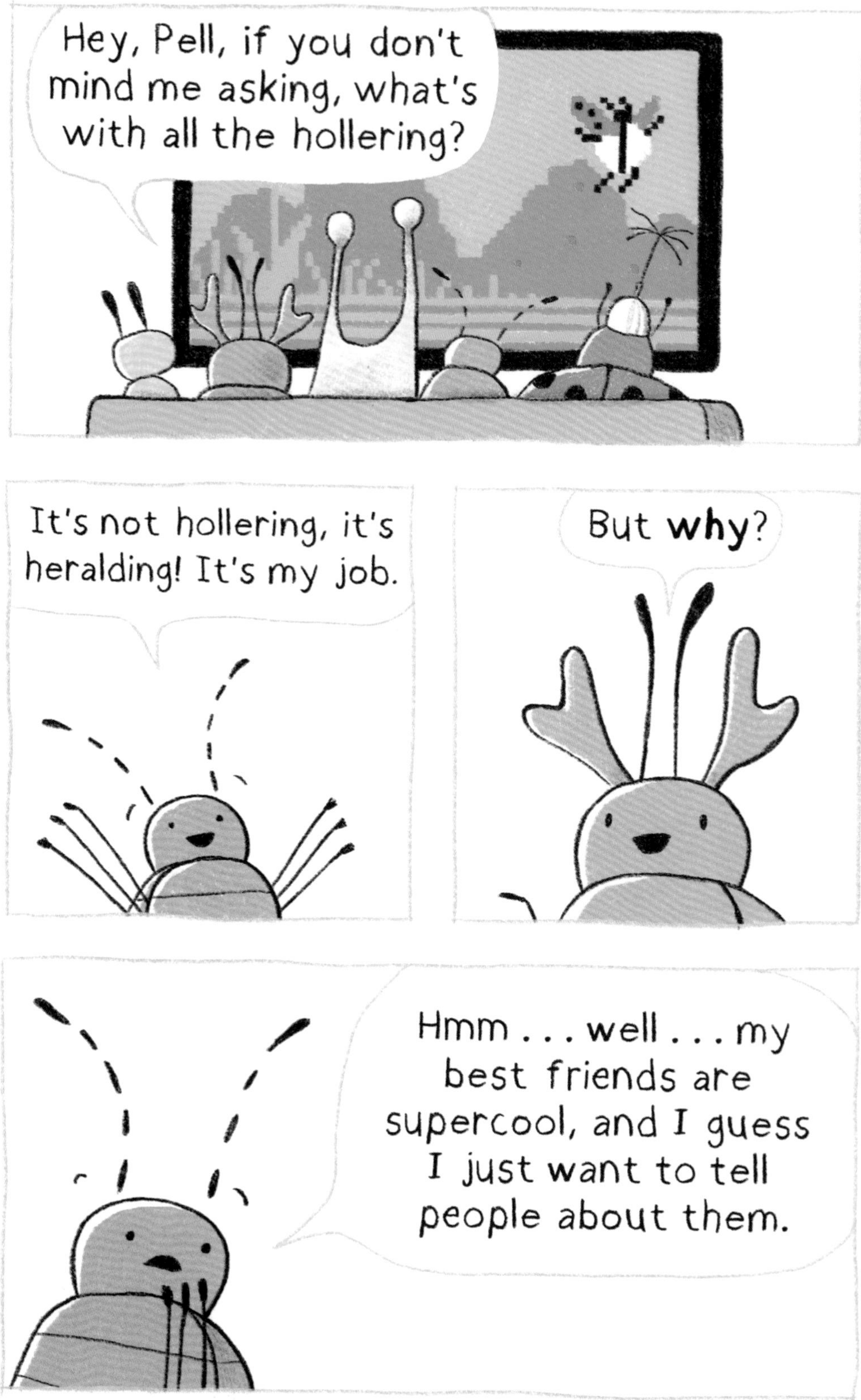
Hey, Pell, if you don't mind me asking, what's with all the hollering?
It's not hollering, it's heralding! It's my job.
But **why**?
Hmm . . . well . . . my best friends are supercool, and I guess I just want to tell people about them.

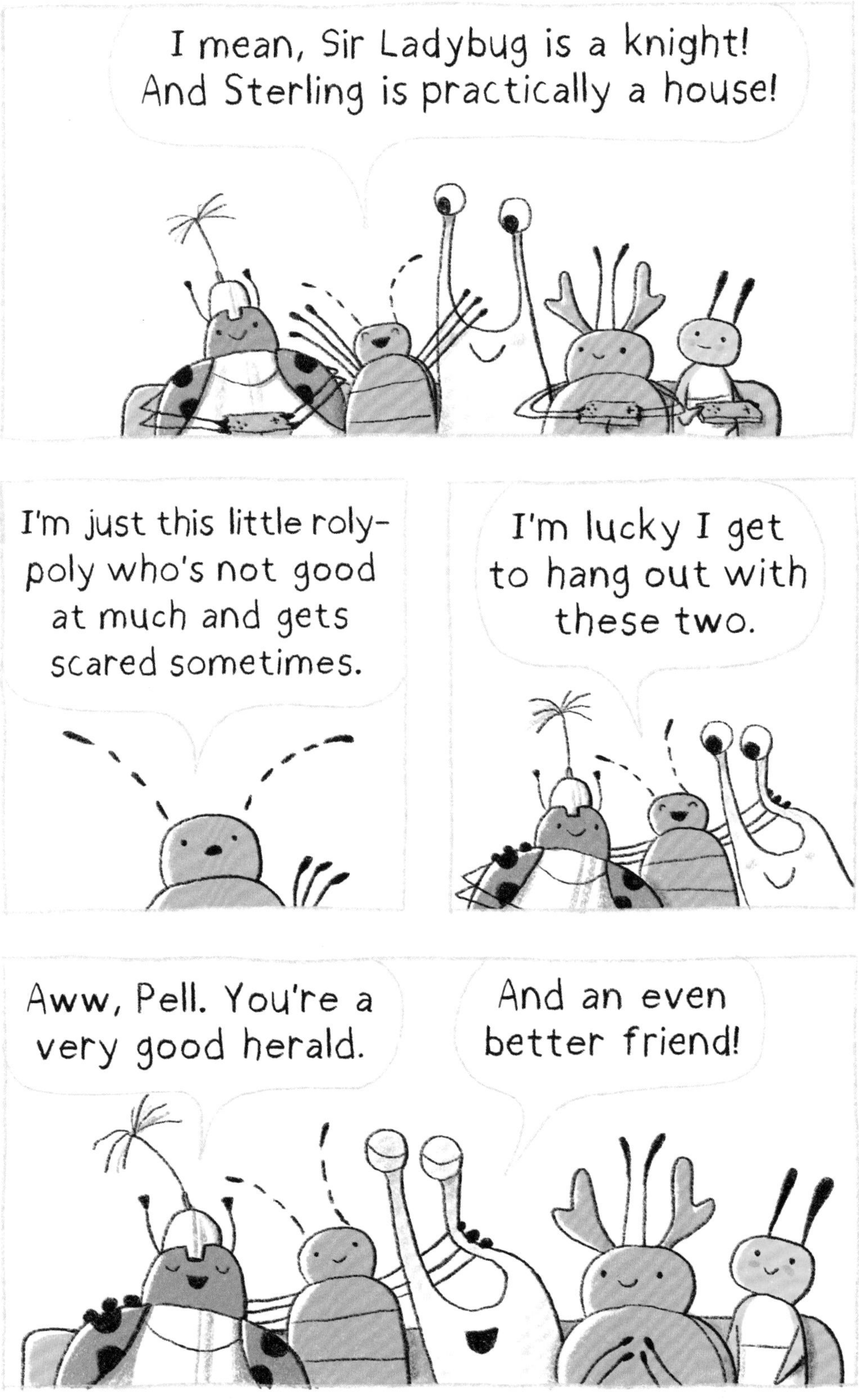
I mean, Sir Ladybug is a knight!
And Sterling is practically a house!
I'm just this little roly-poly who's not good at much and gets scared sometimes.
I'm lucky I get to hang out with these two.
Aww, Pell. You're a very good herald.
And an even better friend!

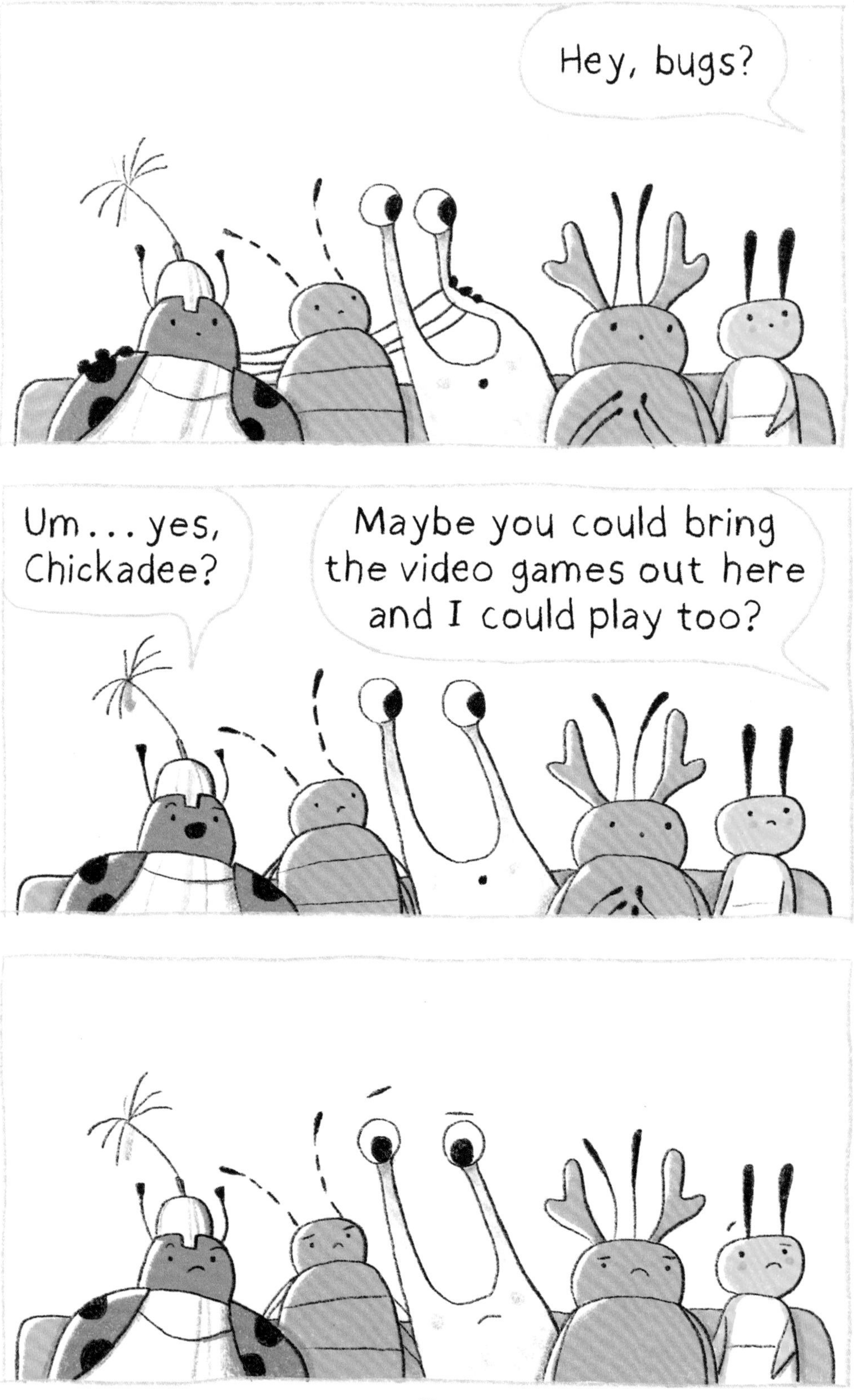
Hey, bugs?
Um . . . yes, Chickadee?
Maybe you could bring the video games out here and I could play too?

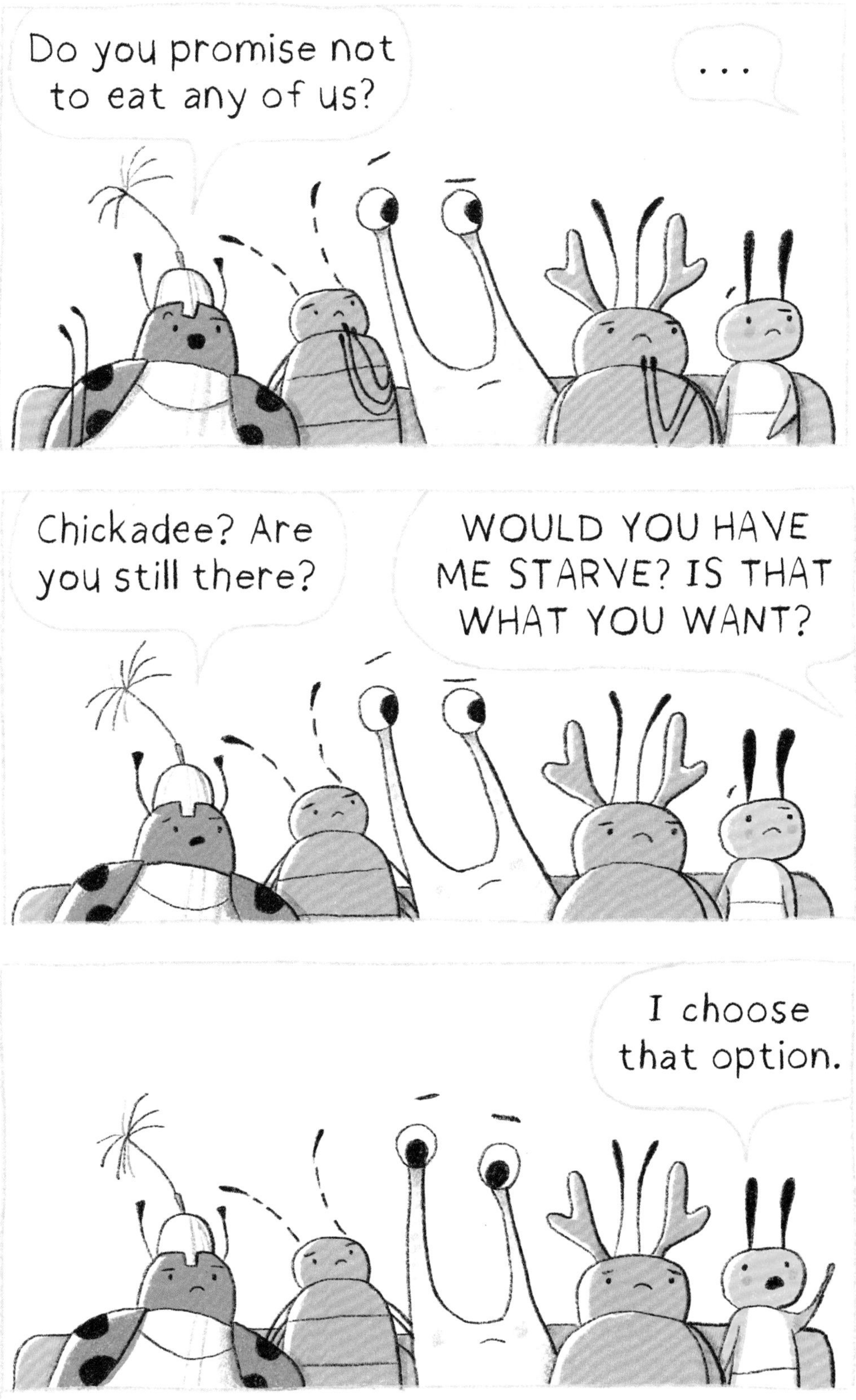
Do you promise not to eat any of us?
...
Chickadee? Are you still there?
WOULD YOU HAVE ME STARVE? IS THAT WHAT YOU WANT?
I choose that option.

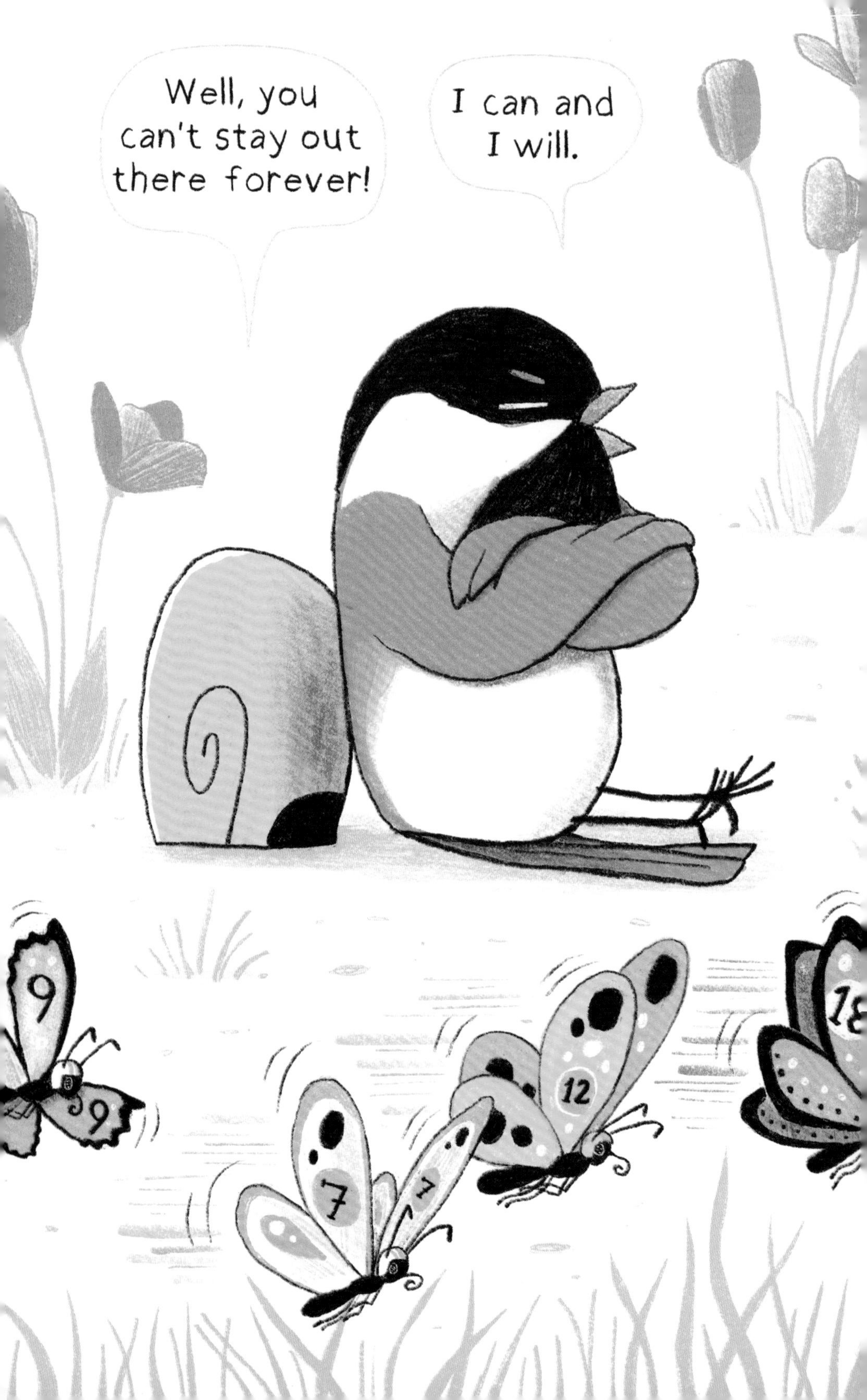
Well, you can't stay out there forever!
I can and I will.
9
9
12
7
7

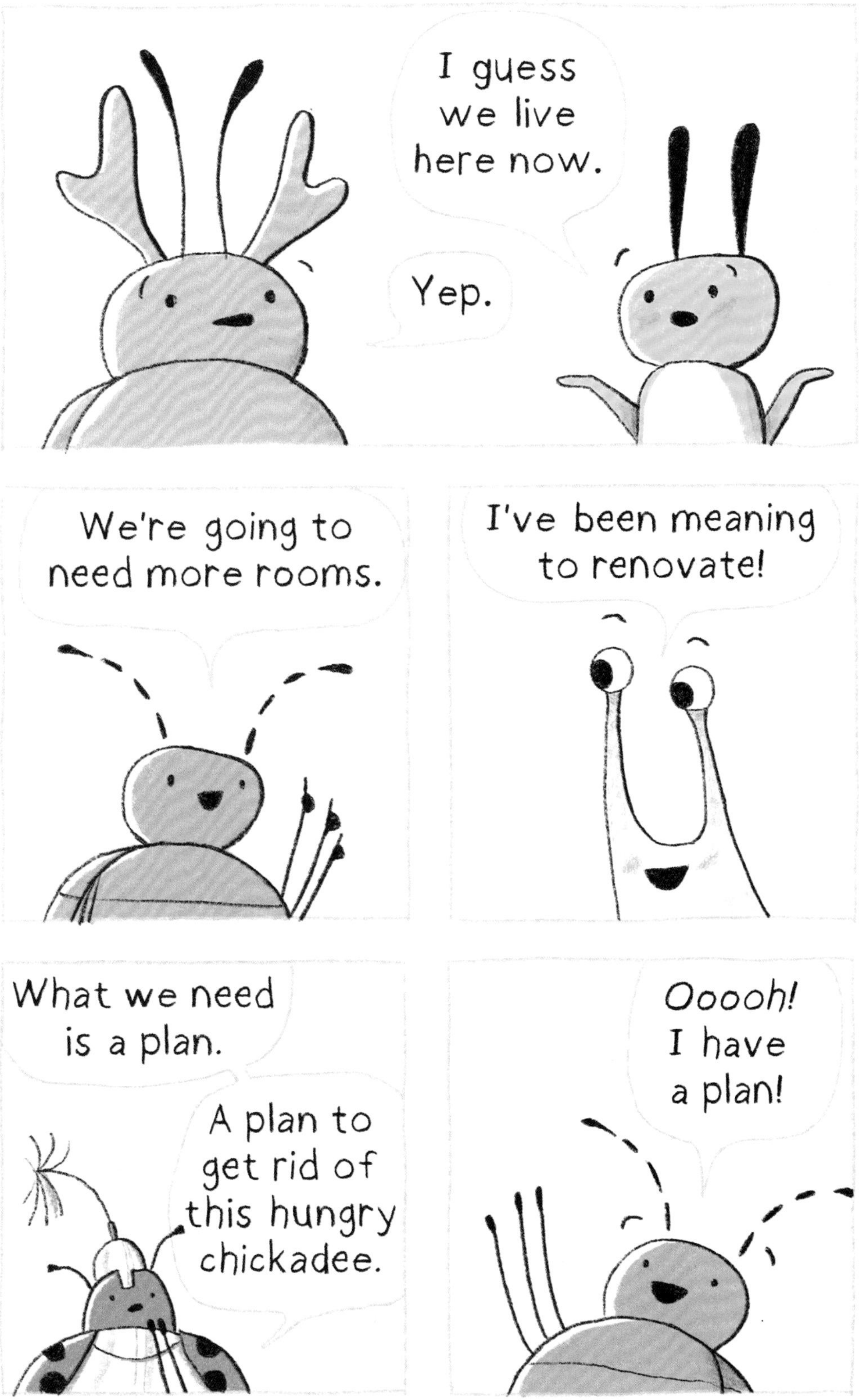
I guess we live here now.
Yep.
We're going to need more rooms.
I've been meaning to renovate!
What we need is a plan.
A plan to get rid of this hungry chickadee.
Ooooh! I have a plan!

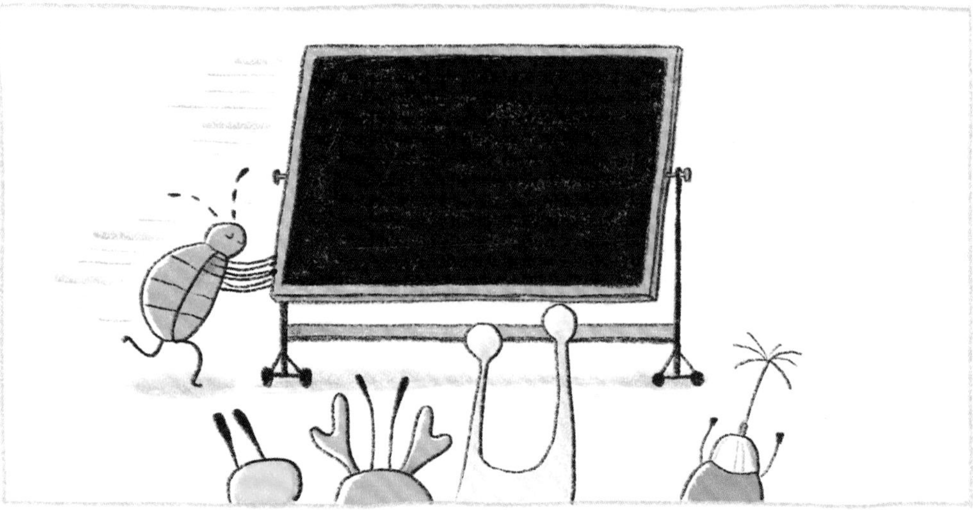

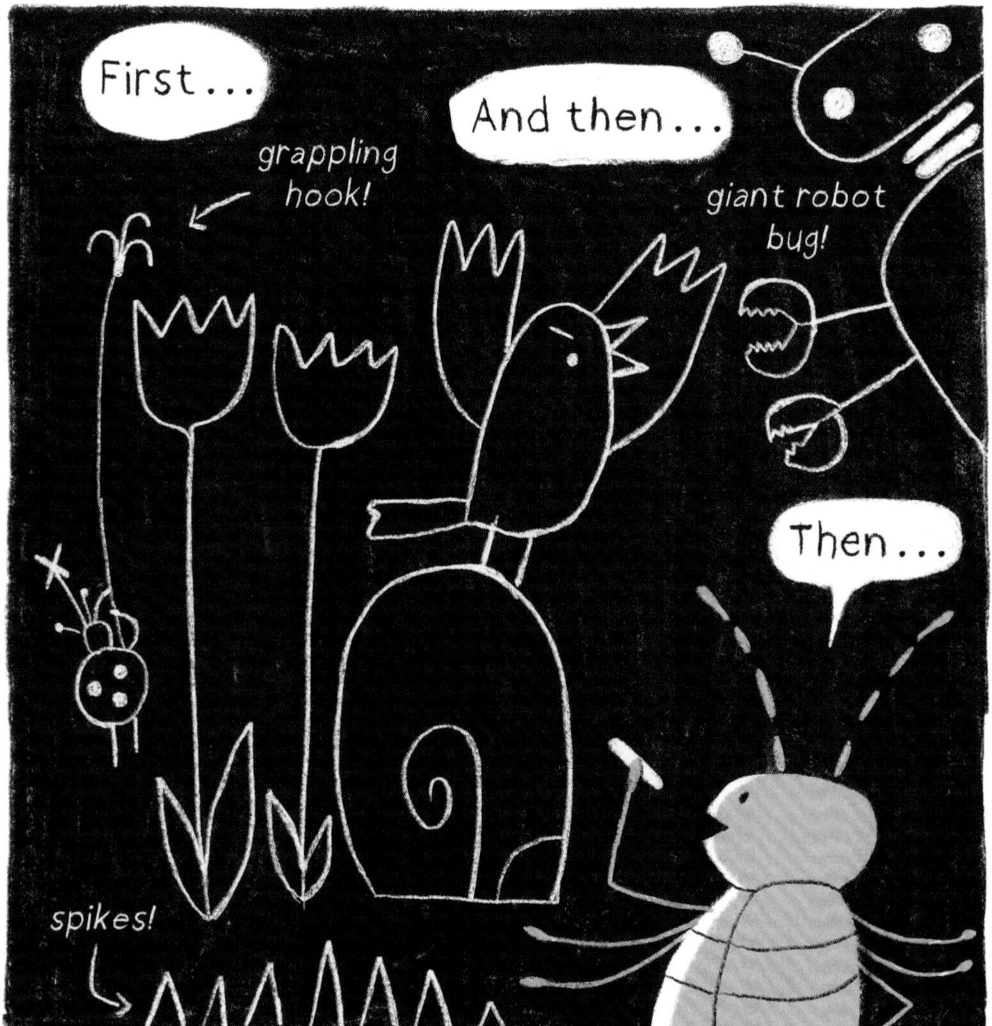
First...
grappling hook!
And then...
giant robot bug!
Then...
spikes!

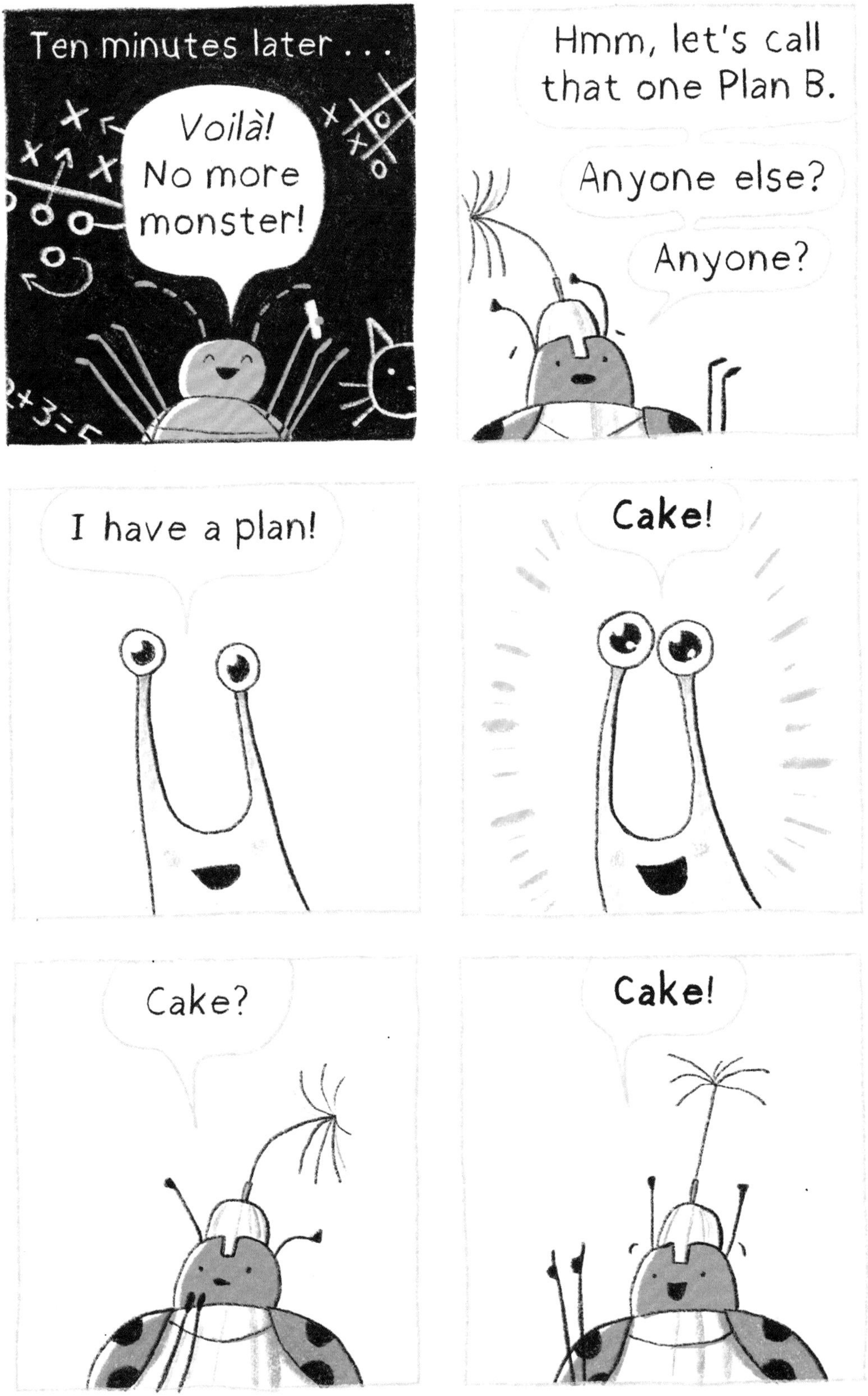
Ten minutes later . . .
Voilà! No more monster!
Hmm, let's call that one Plan B.
Anyone else?
Anyone?
I have a plan!
Cake!
Cake?
Cake!

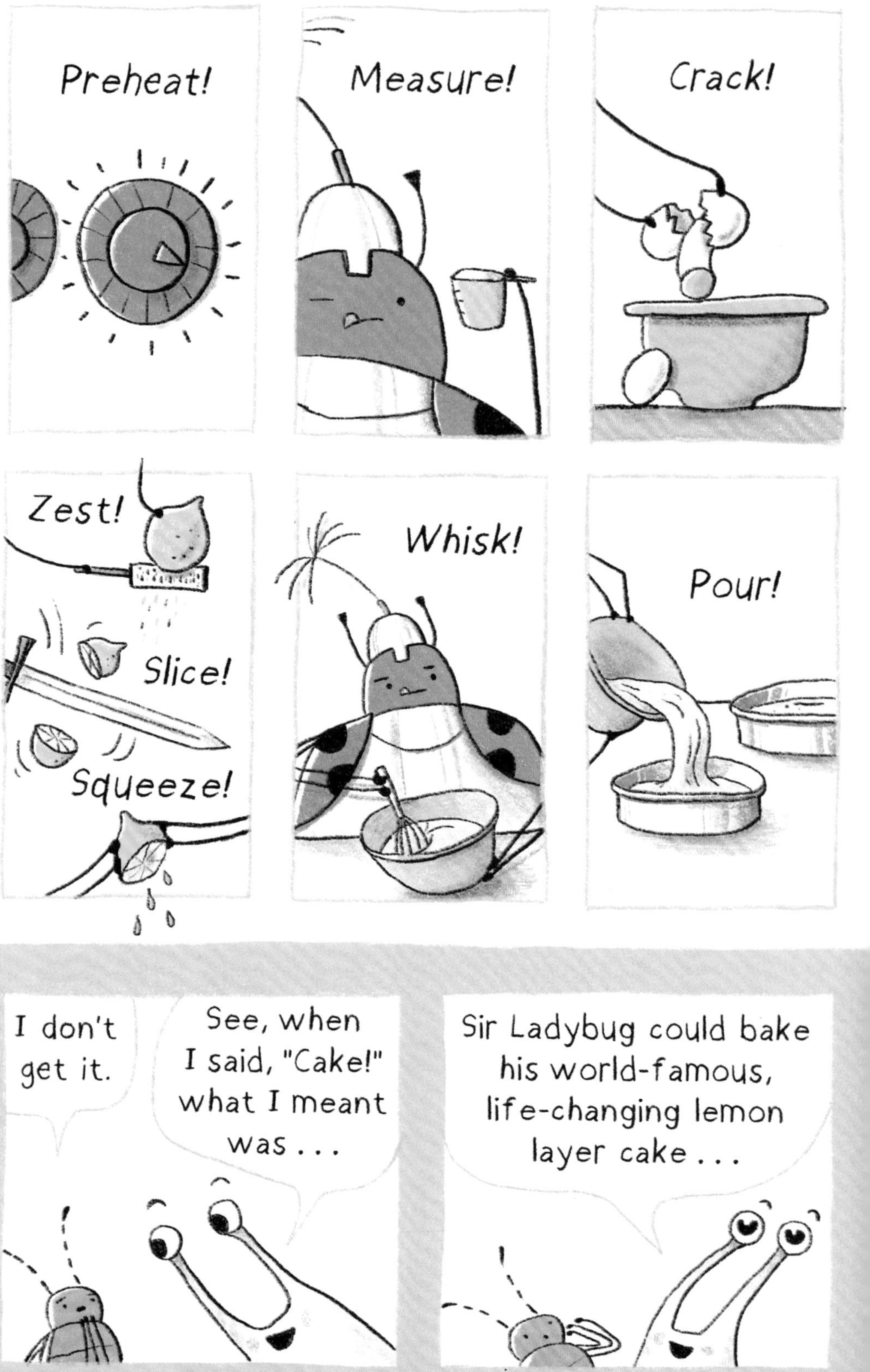
Preheat!
Measure!
Crack!
Zest!
Slice!
Squeeze!
Whisk!
Pour!
I don't get it.
See, when I said, "Cake!" what I meant was . . .
Sir Ladybug could bake his world-famous, life-changing lemon layer cake . . .

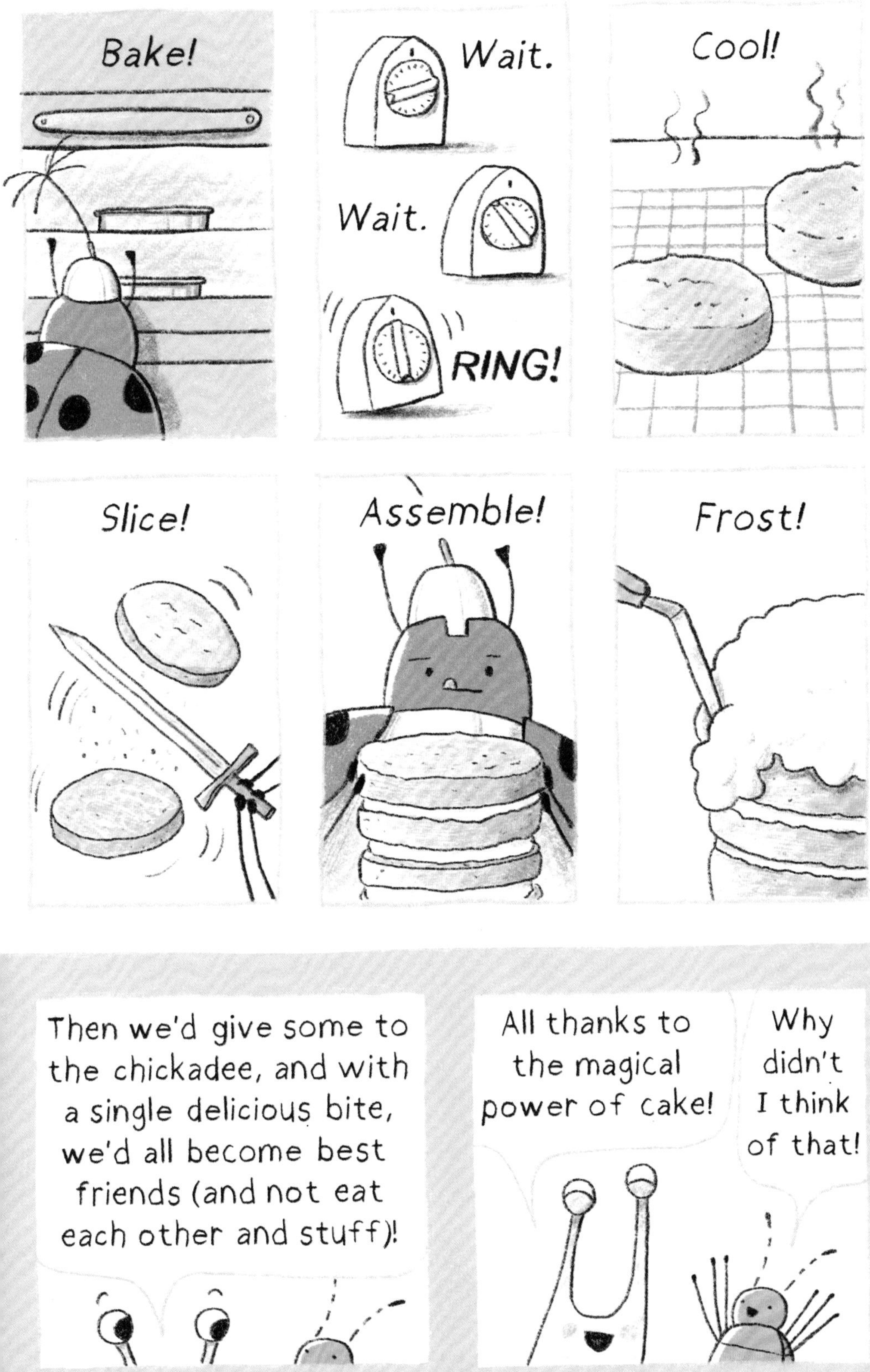

Bake!
Wait.
Wait.
RING!
Cool!
Slice!
Assemble!
Frost!
Then we'd give some to the chickadee, and with a single delicious bite, we'd all become best friends (and not eat each other and stuff)!
All thanks to the magical power of cake!
Why didn't I think of that!

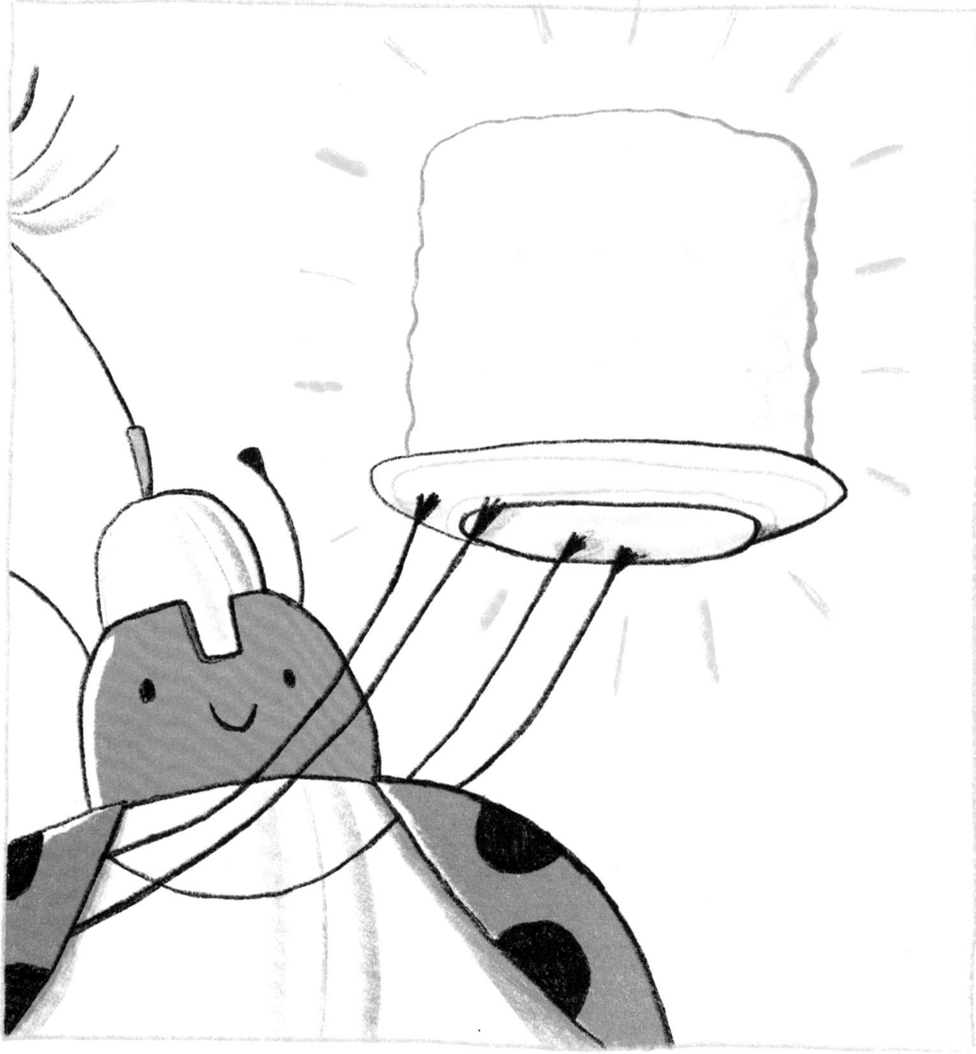

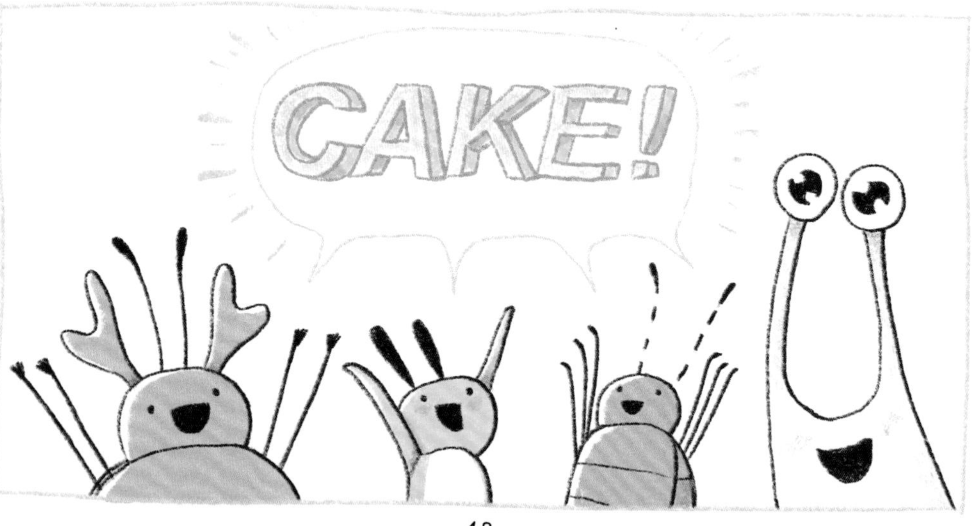
CAKE!

Interlude: Sterling's Poem

The Slice of Cake

so much depends
upon

a slice of
cake

glazed with thick
frosting

beside the video game
console.

Beautiful.

Chapter 4: Cake!

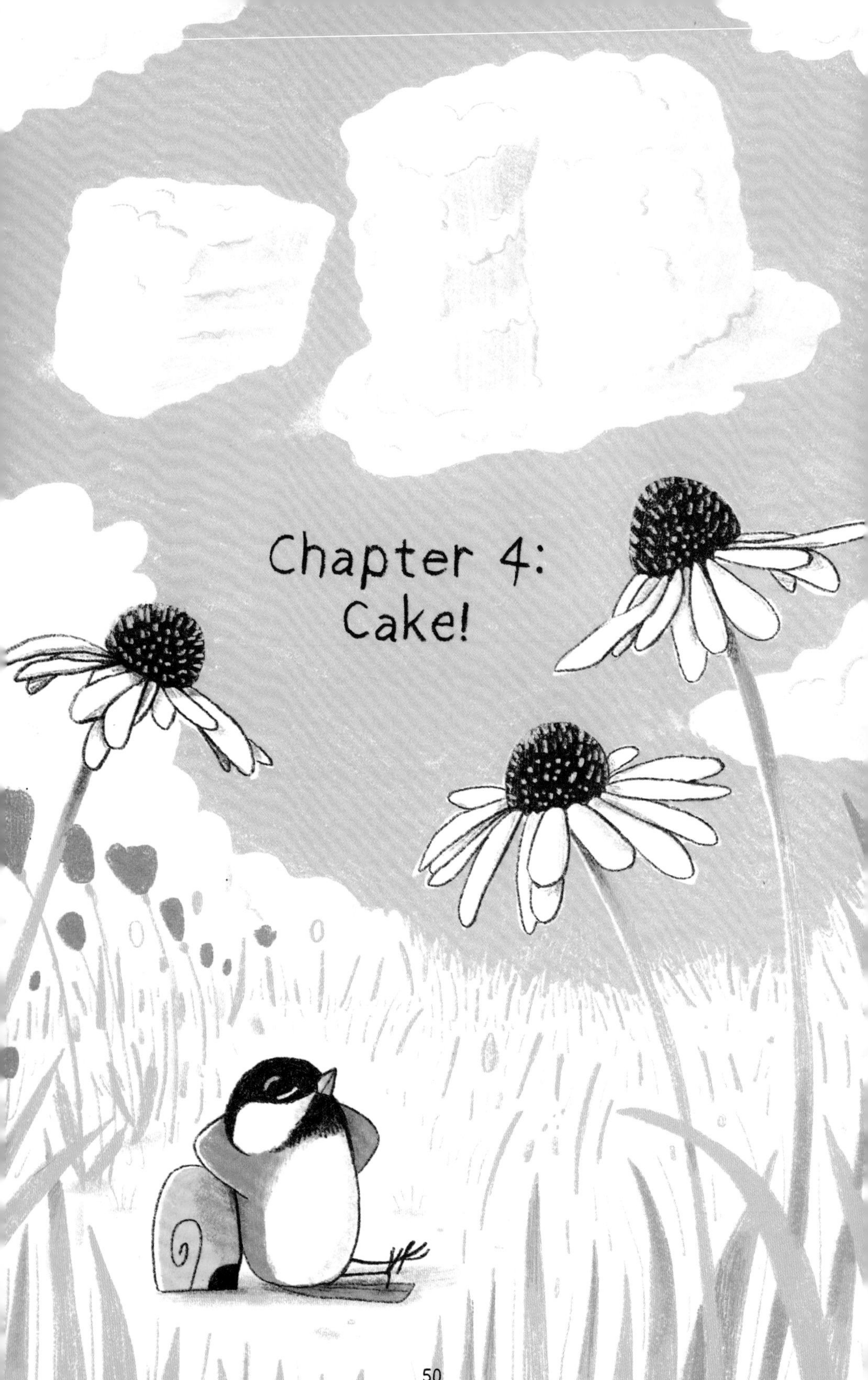

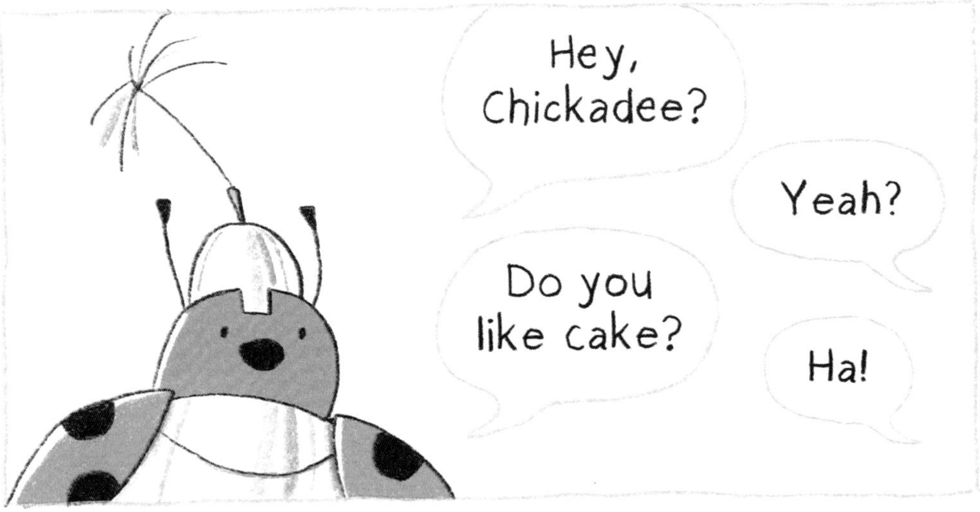
Hey, Chickadee?
Yeah?
Do you like cake?
Ha!

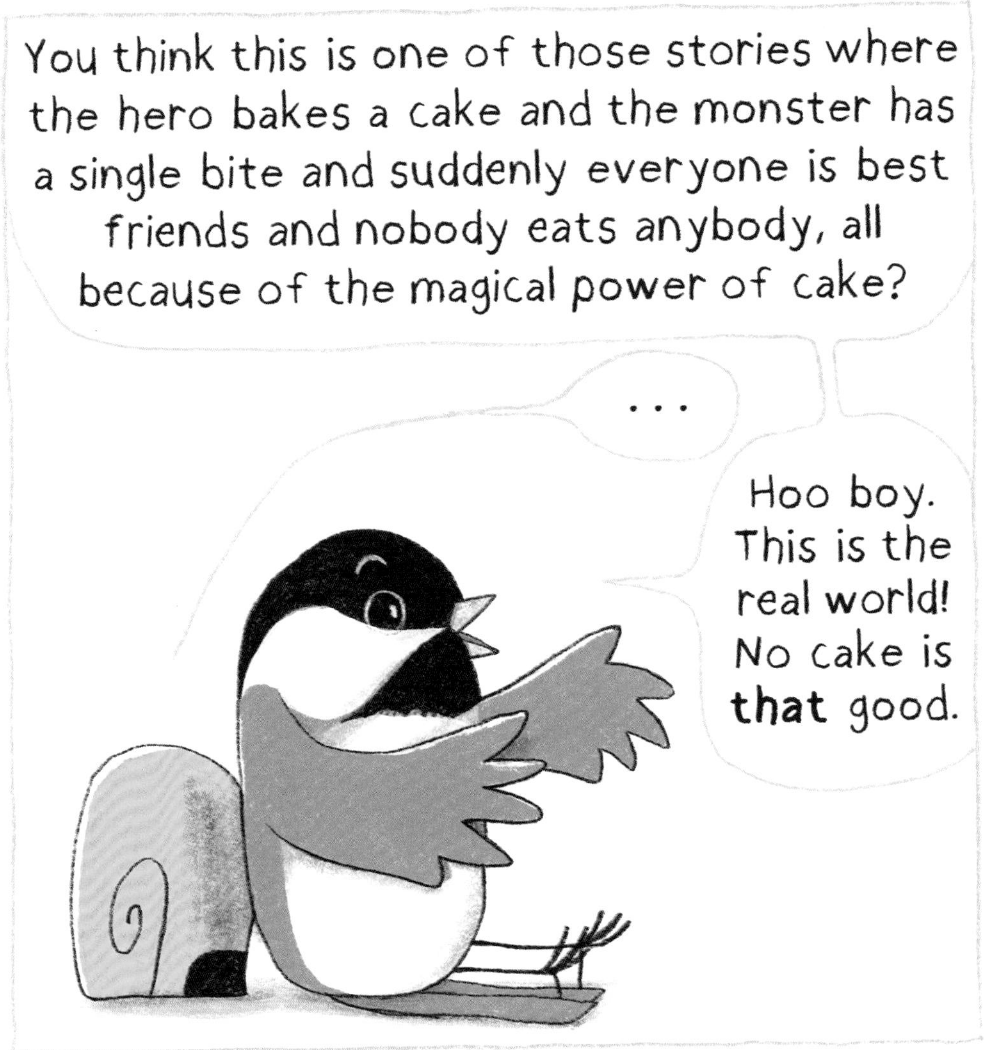
You think this is one of those stories where the hero bakes a cake and the monster has a single bite and suddenly everyone is best friends and nobody eats anybody, all because of the magical power of cake?
. . .
Hoo boy. This is the real world! No cake is **that** good.

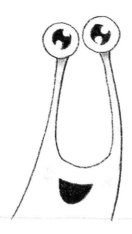

You've never tasted *Sir Ladybug's Lemon Layer Cake!*

 Hmm...

How do I know this isn't a trap? You'll distract me with your cake and poke me with your sword!

How dare you besmudge my knightly honor!

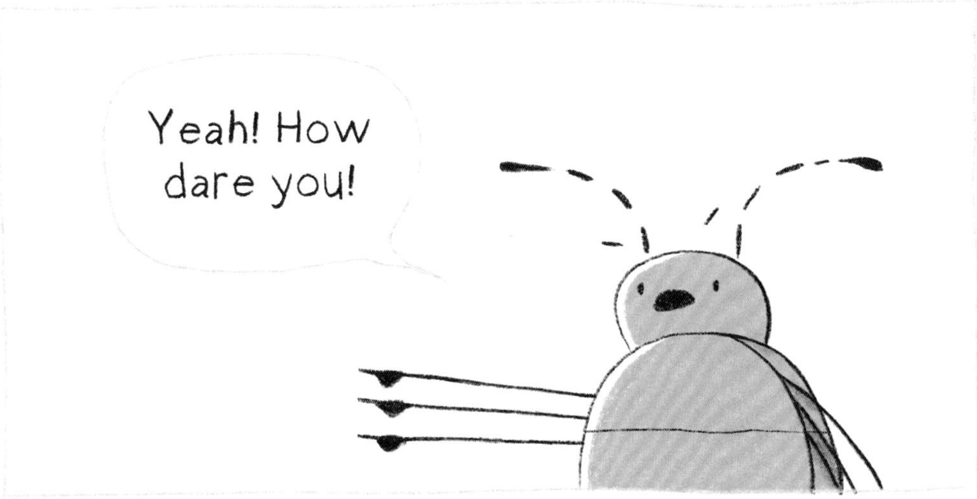
Yeah! How dare you!

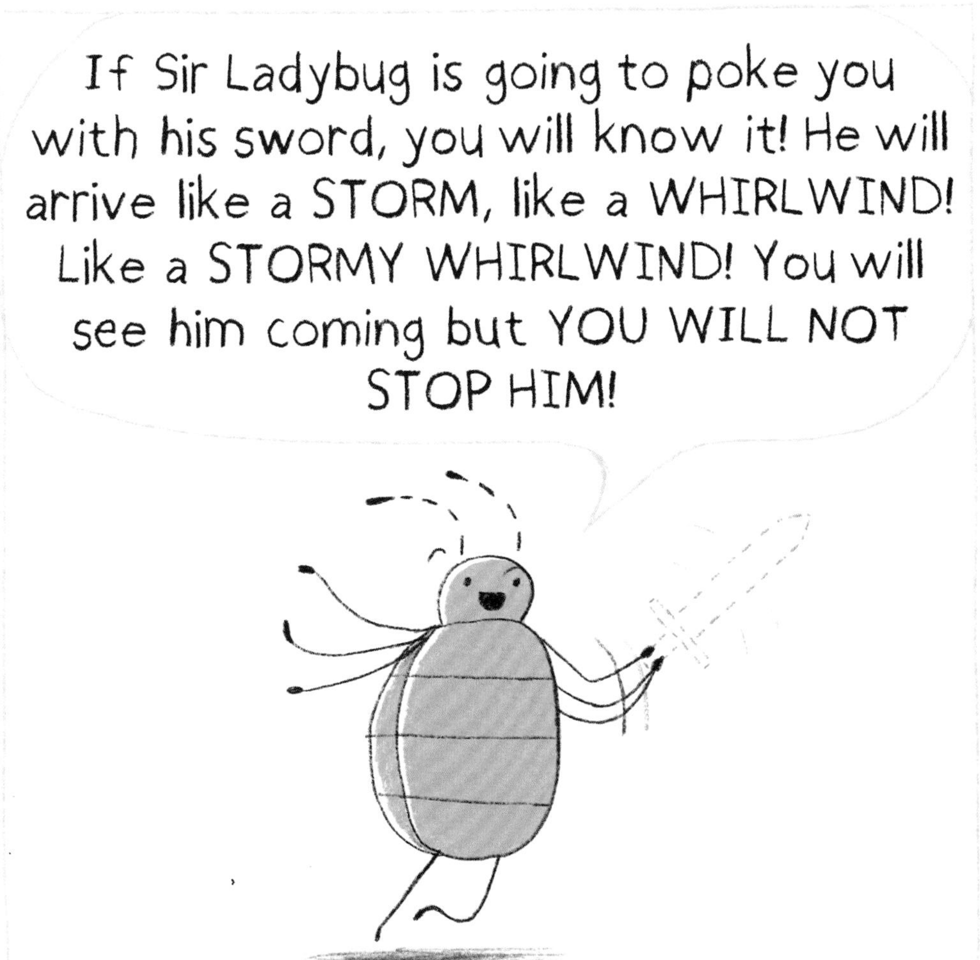
If Sir Ladybug is going to poke you with his sword, you will know it! He will arrive like a STORM, like a WHIRLWIND! Like a STORMY WHIRLWIND! You will see him coming but YOU WILL NOT STOP HIM!

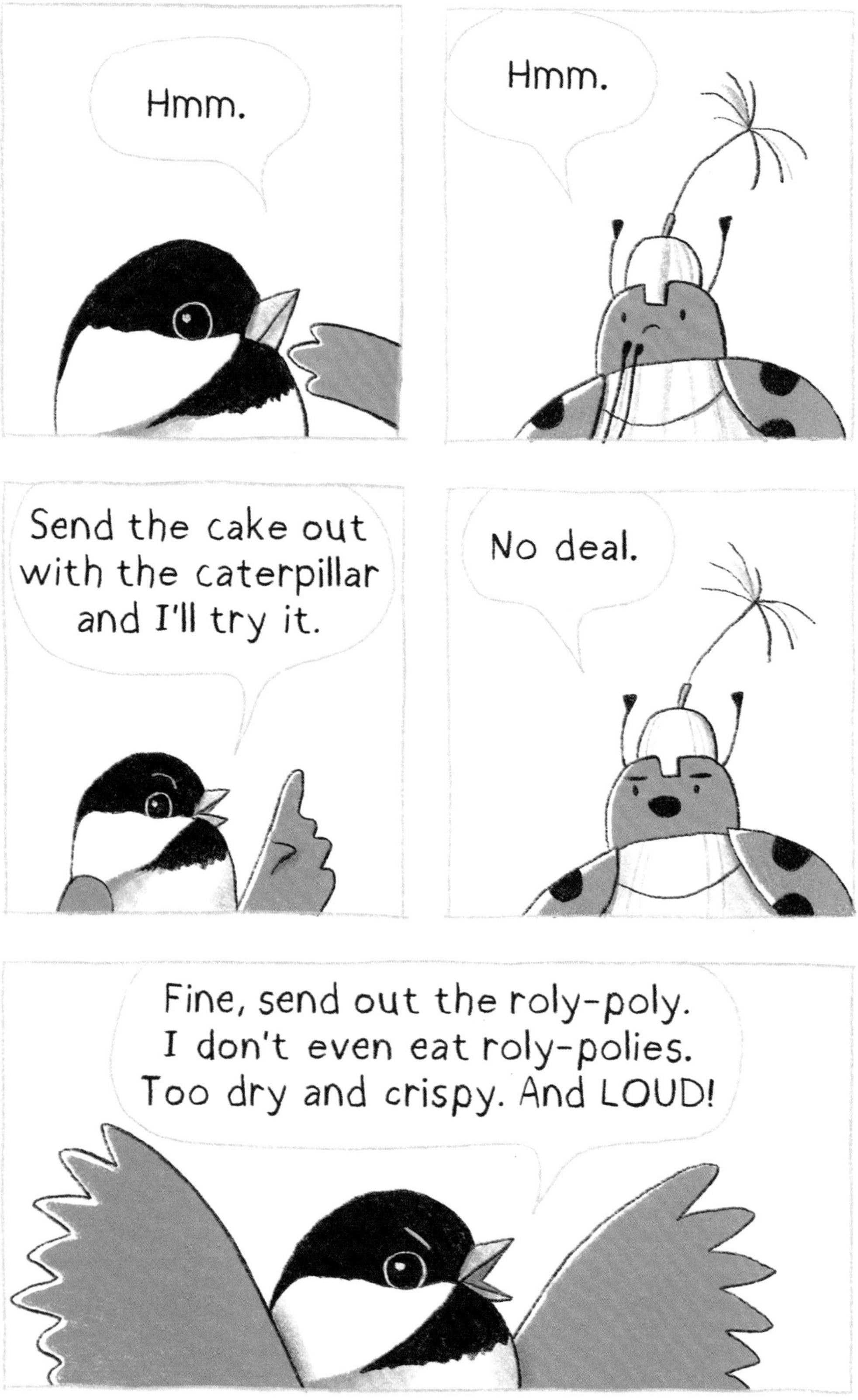
Hmm.
Hmm.
Send the cake out with the caterpillar and I'll try it.
No deal.
Fine, send out the roly-poly. I don't even eat roly-polies. Too dry and crispy. And LOUD!

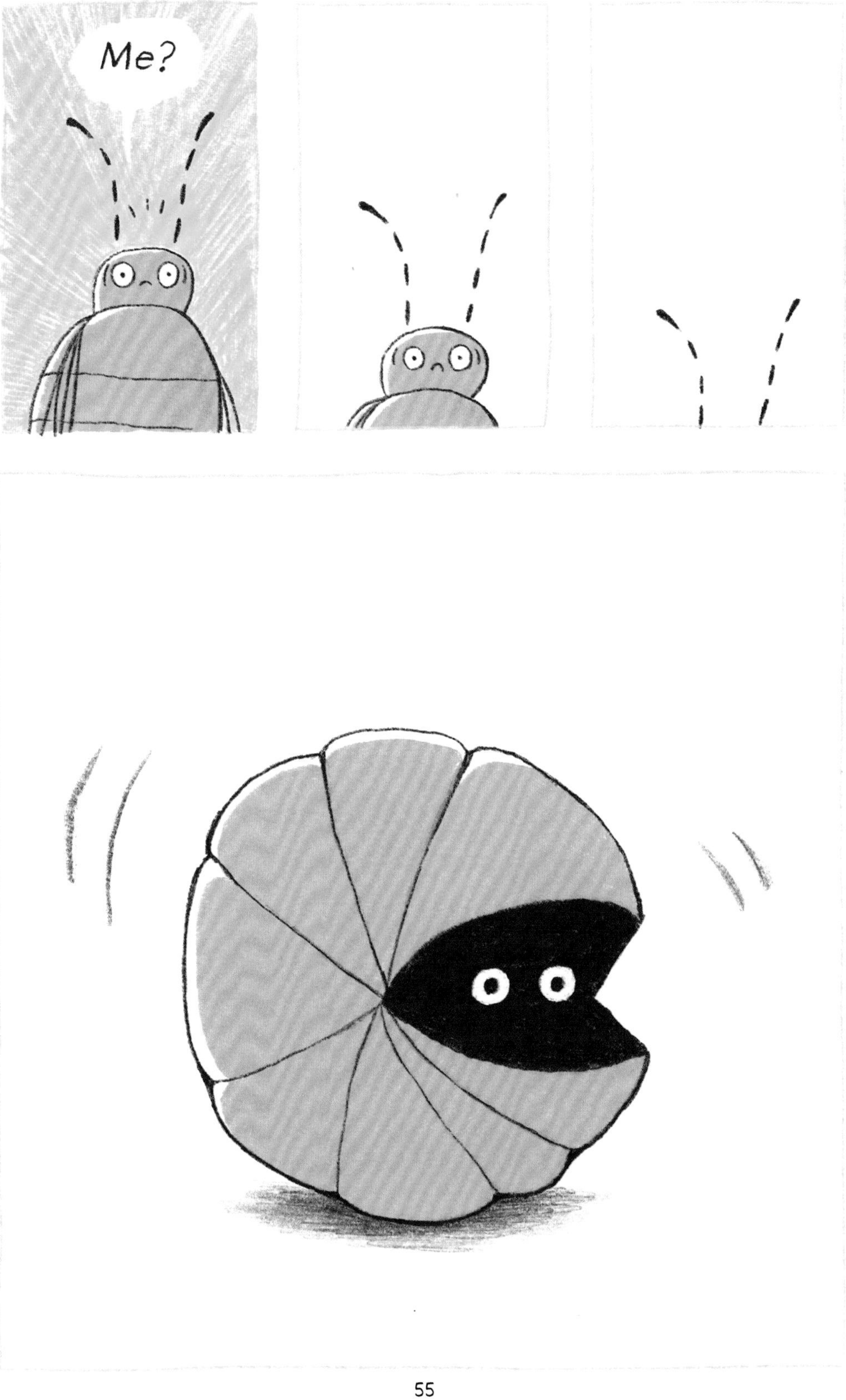
Me?

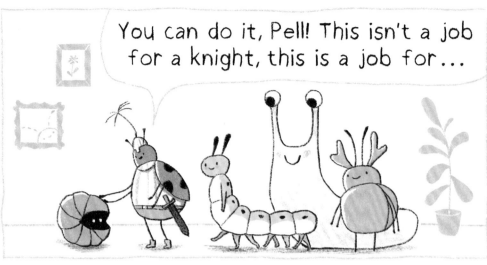

You can do it, Pell! This isn't a job for a knight, this is a job for...

THE WORLD'S BEST HERALD!

YEAH!!!

But... I'm not as brave as you, Sir Ladybug.

Hmm...

There are lots of different kinds of brave.

There's fight-with-a-sword brave...

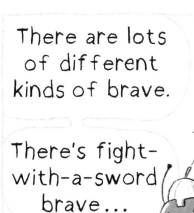

...and there's stand-in-front-of-people-and-talk brave.

You know, sometimes *I* wish I were as brave as **you**.

Really?

Really really.

POP

Okay! I'll do it!

Cake me!

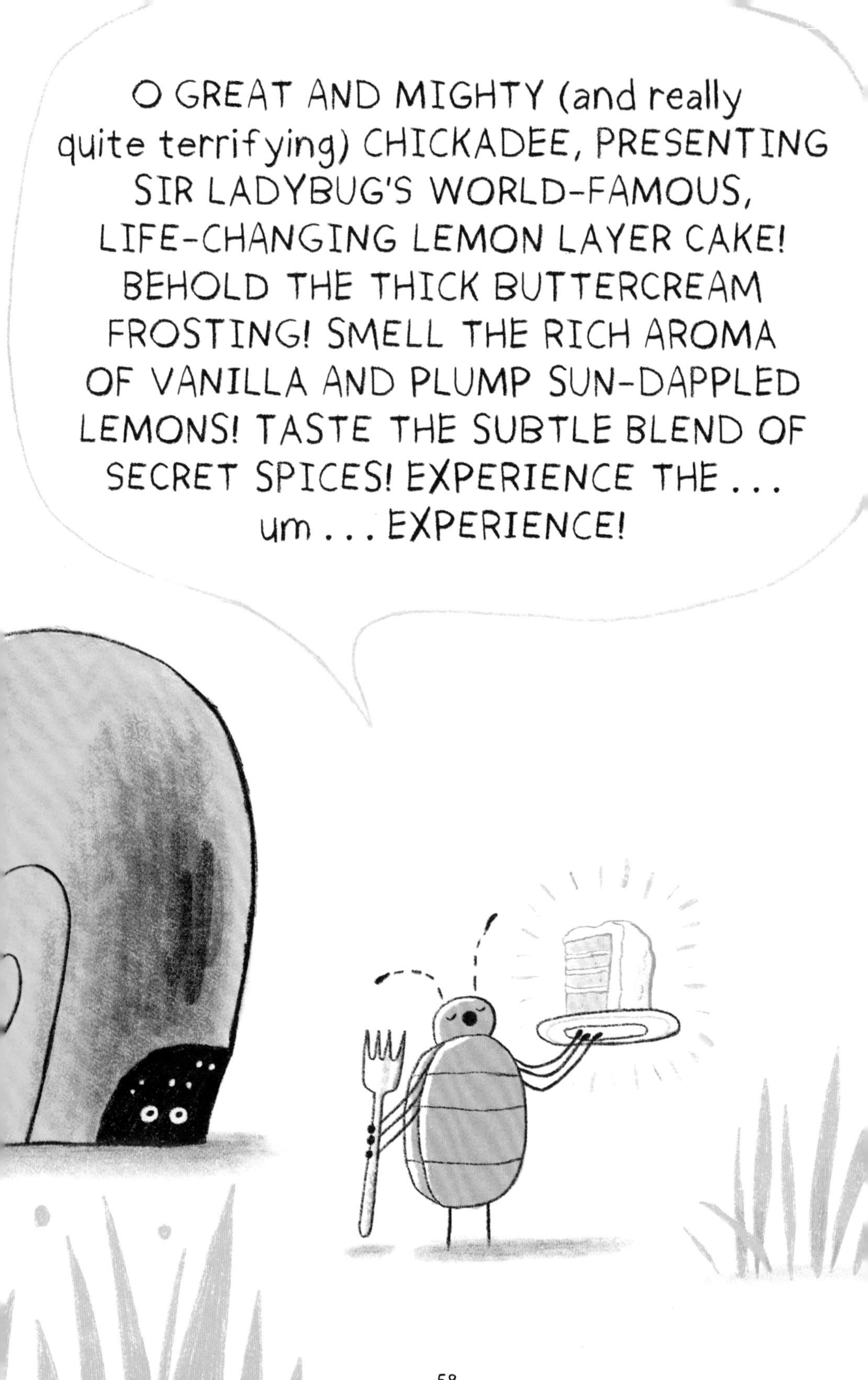
O GREAT AND MIGHTY (and really quite terrifying) CHICKADEE, PRESENTING SIR LADYBUG'S WORLD-FAMOUS, LIFE-CHANGING LEMON LAYER CAKE! BEHOLD THE THICK BUTTERCREAM FROSTING! SMELL THE RICH AROMA OF VANILLA AND PLUMP SUN-DAPPLED LEMONS! TASTE THE SUBTLE BLEND OF SECRET SPICES! EXPERIENCE THE . . . um . . . EXPERIENCE!

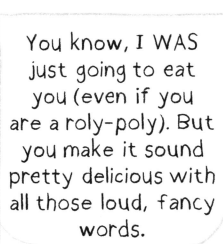

You know, I WAS just going to eat you (even if you are a roly-poly). But you make it sound pretty delicious with all those loud, fancy words.

All right, I'll try the cake.

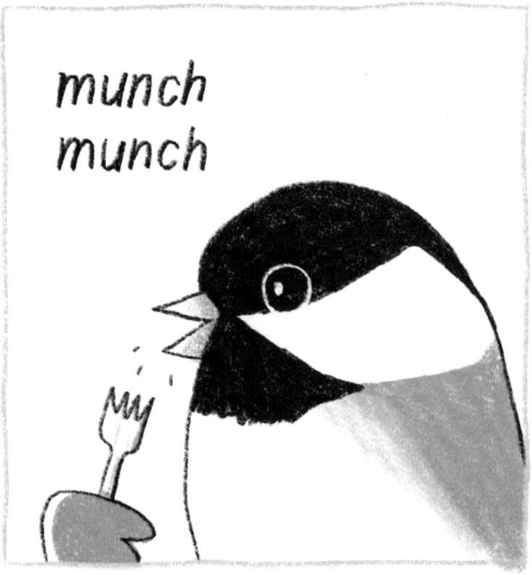
munch
munch

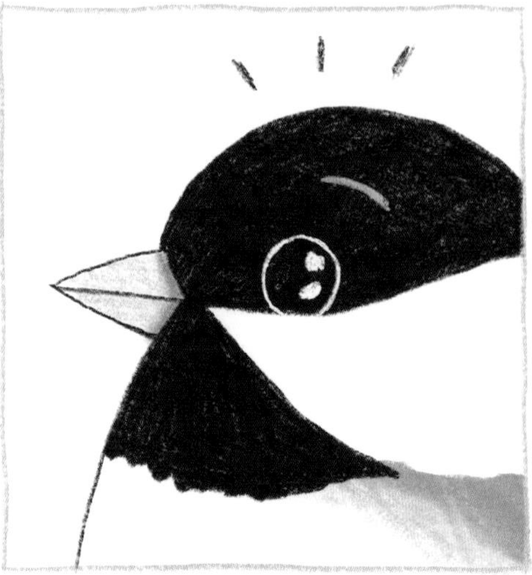

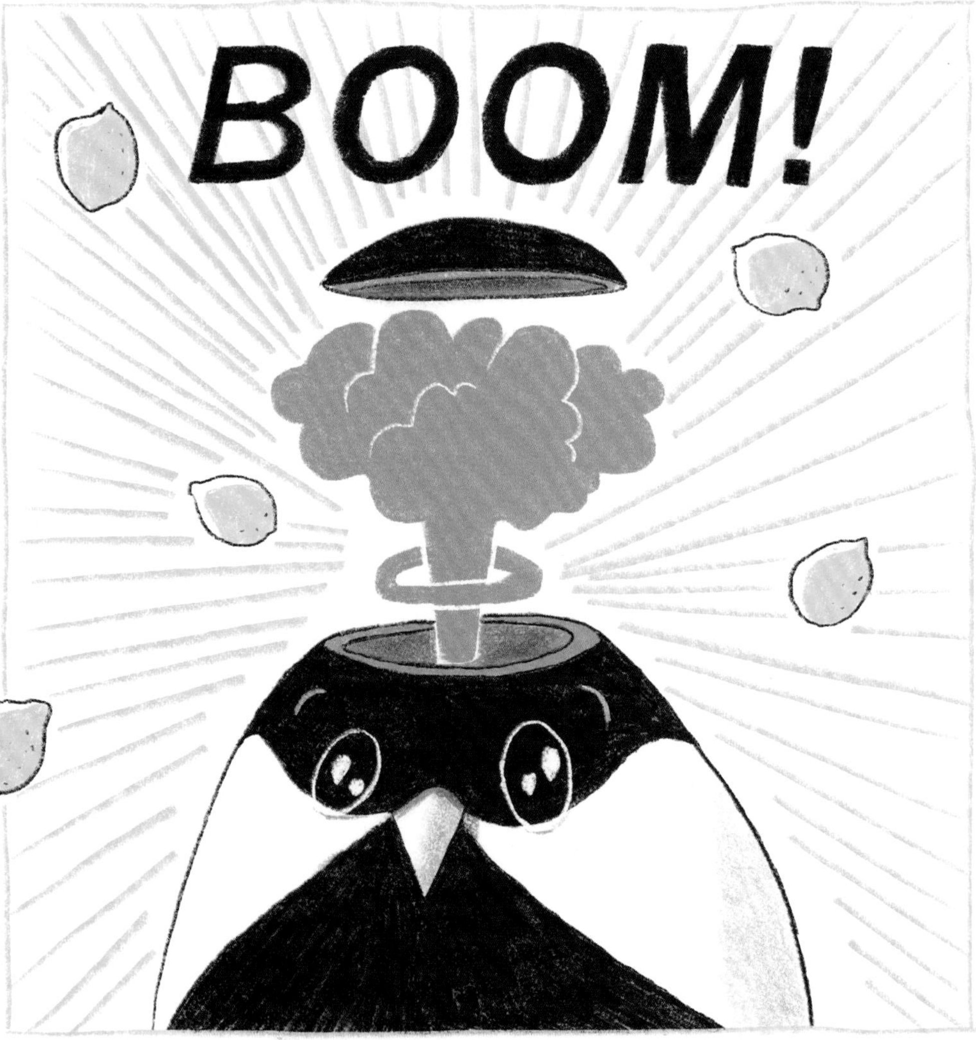
BOOM!

fwump

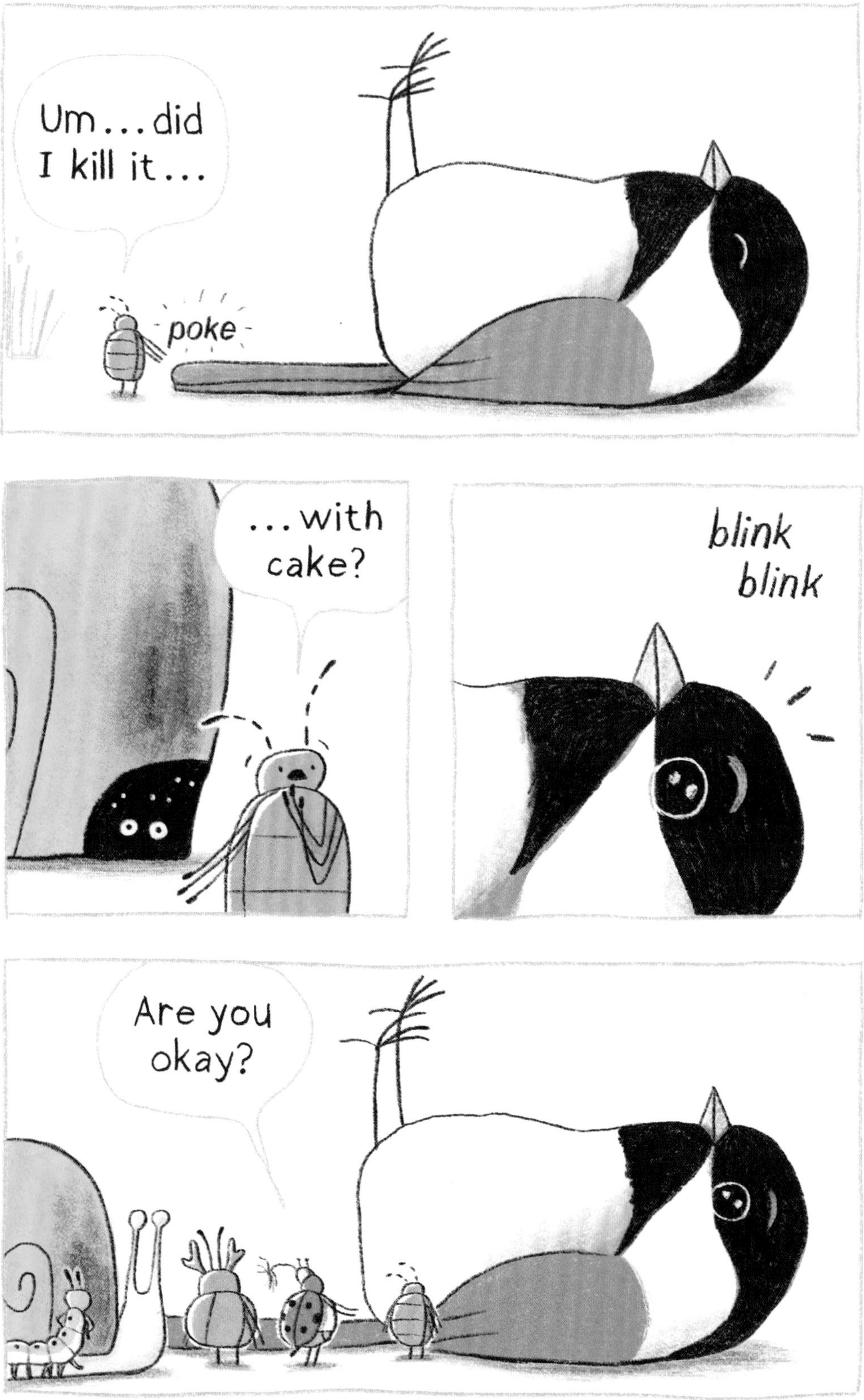
Um...did I kill it...
poke
...with cake?
blink blink
Are you okay?

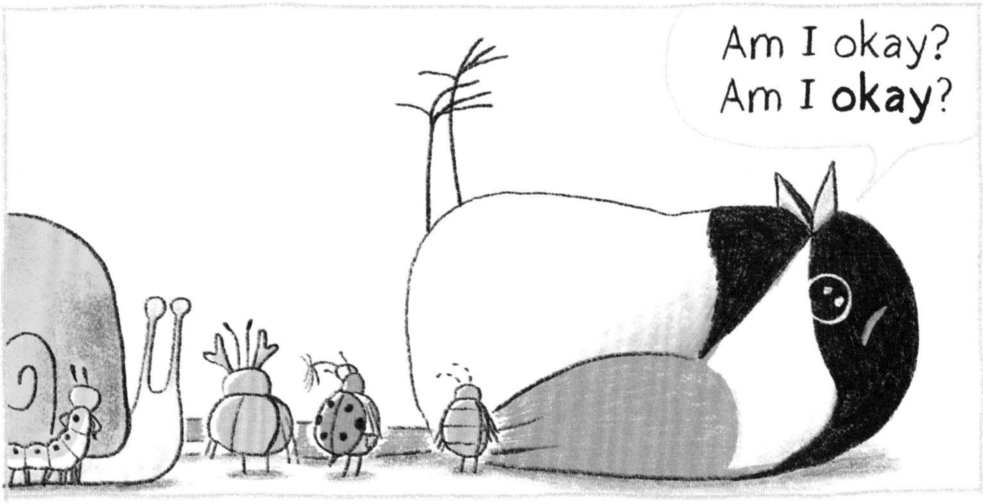
Am I okay?
Am I **okay**?

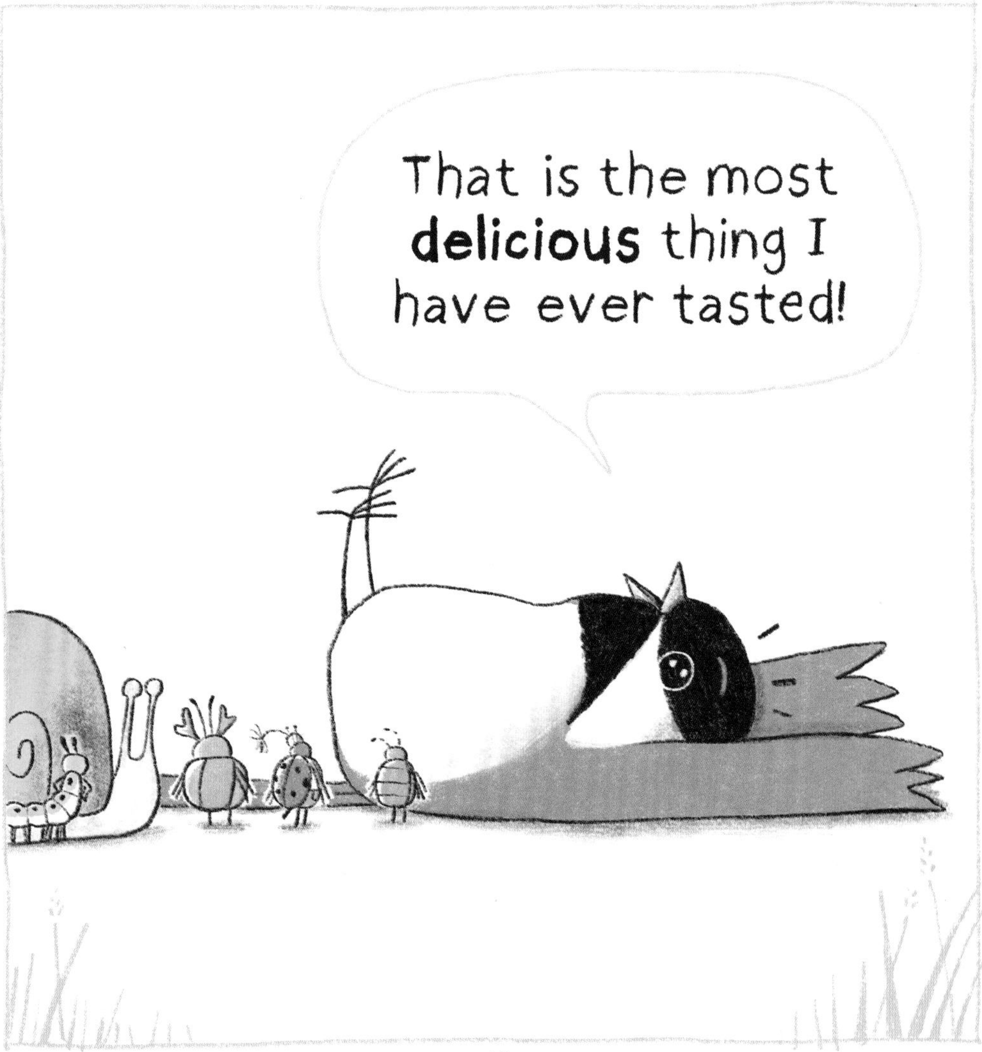
That is the most **delicious** thing I have ever tasted!

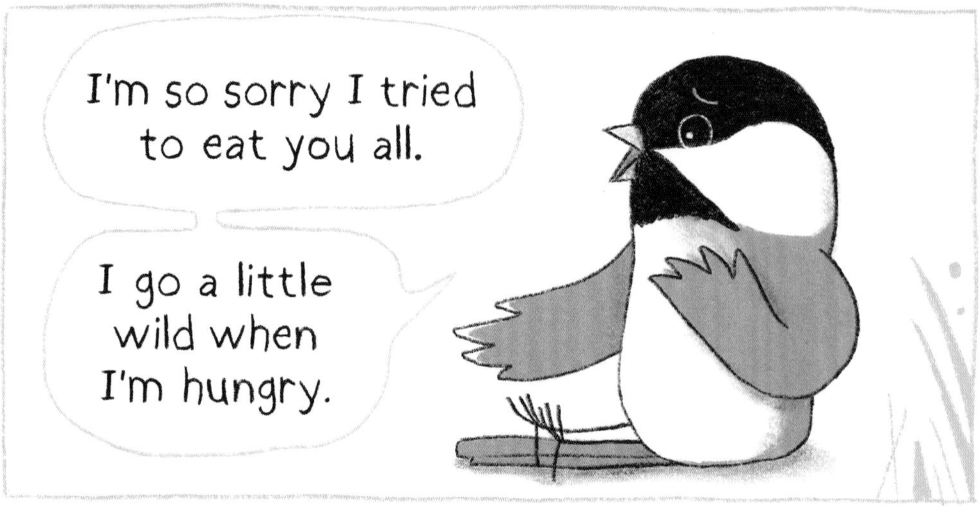
I'm so sorry I tried to eat you all.
I go a little wild when I'm hungry.

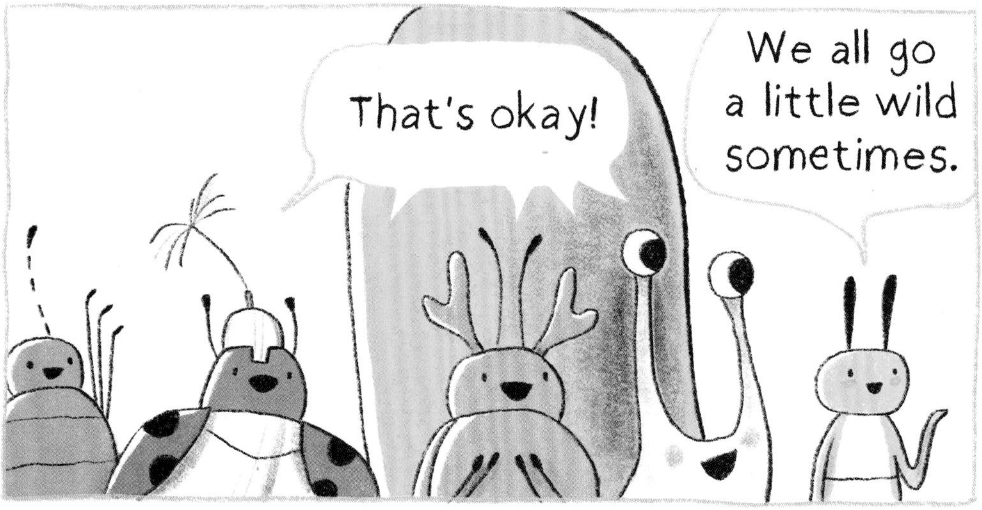
That's okay!
We all go a little wild sometimes.

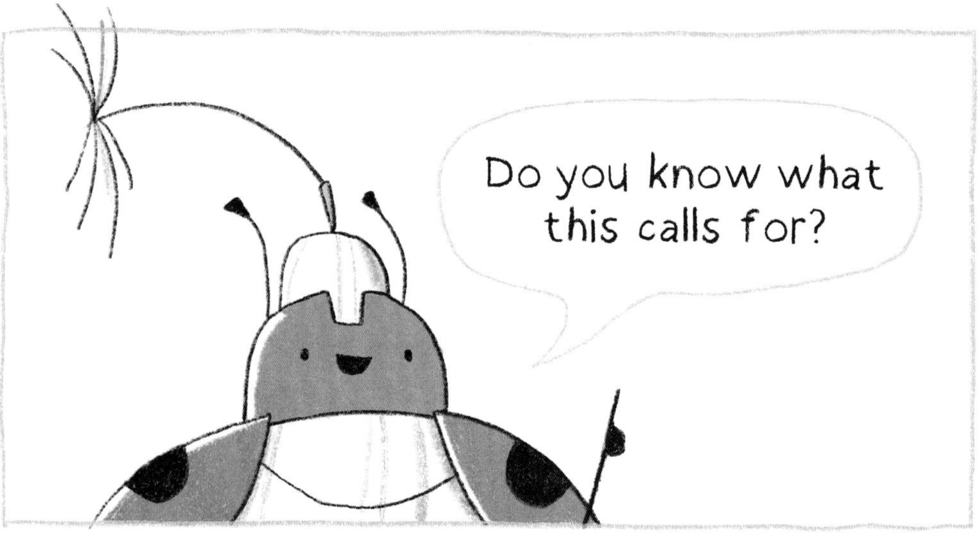
Do you know what this calls for?

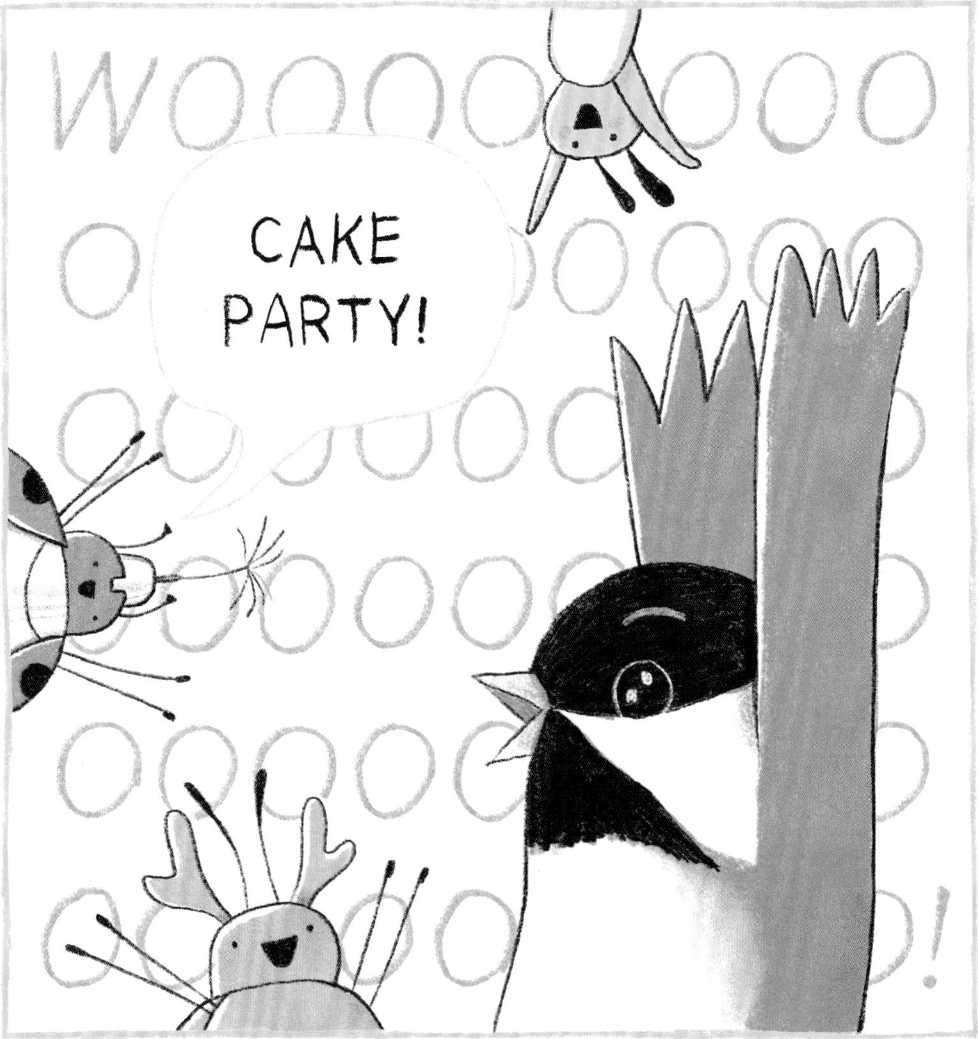
WOOOOOOOOOOOOOOOOOOOOOOOOOOOOOO!
CAKE PARTY!

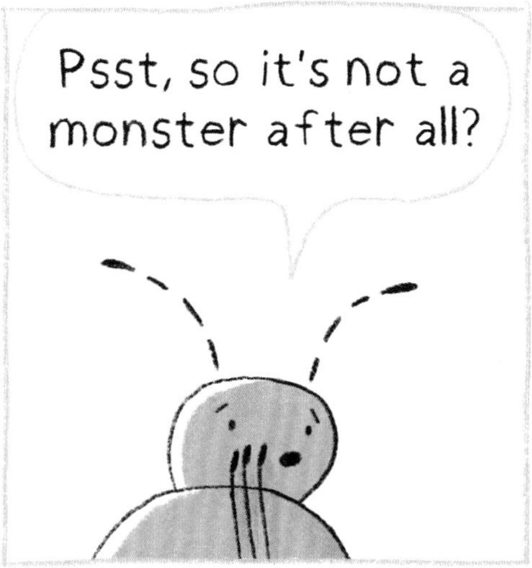
Psst, so it's not a monster after all?

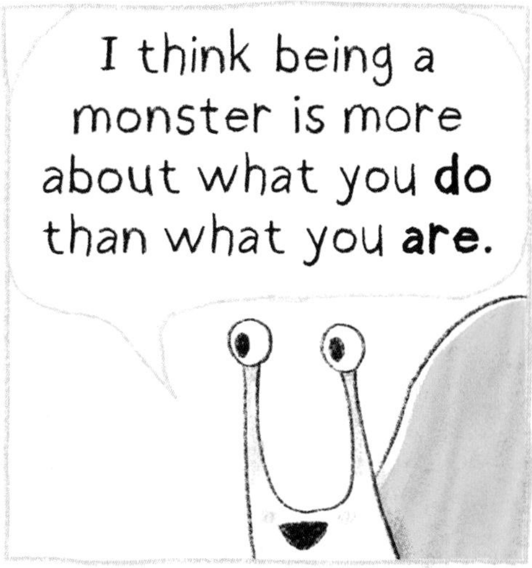
I think being a monster is more about what you **do** than what you **are**.

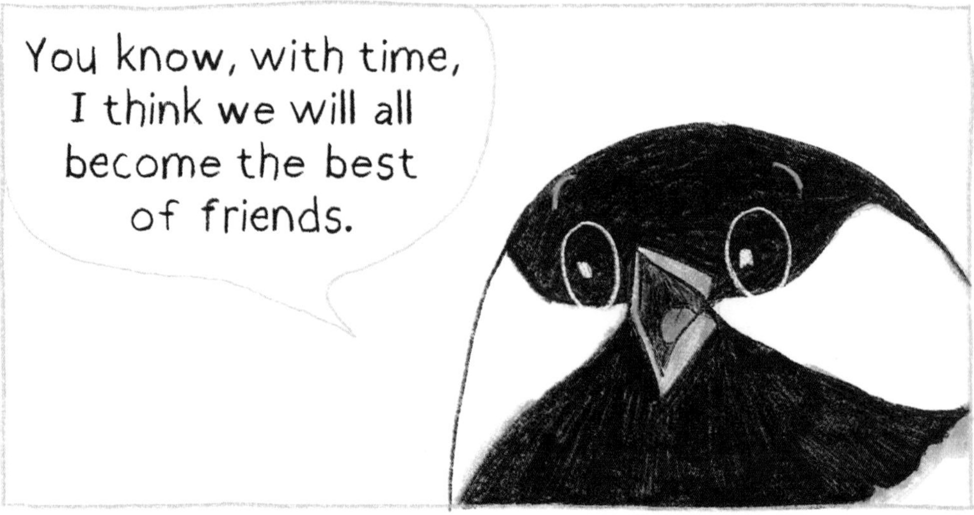
You know, with time, I think we will all become the best of friends.

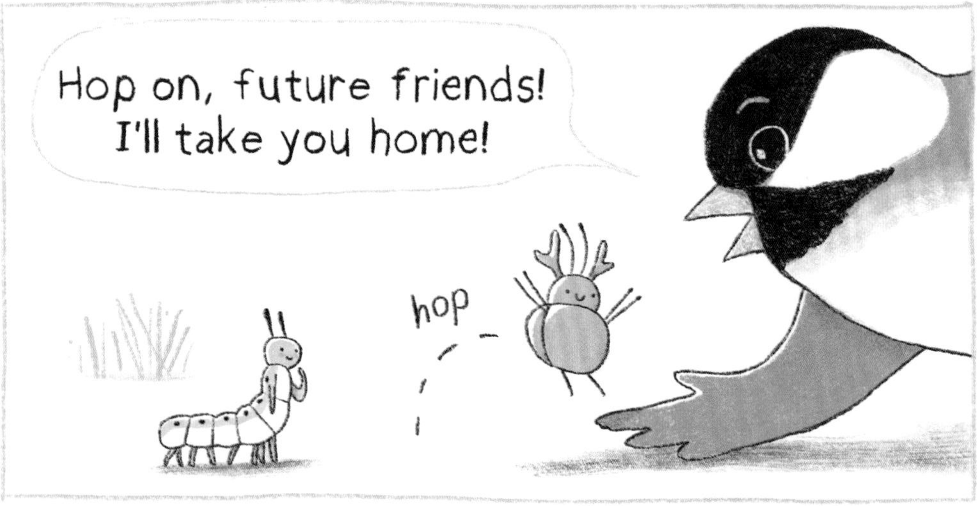
Hop on, future friends! I'll take you home!
hop

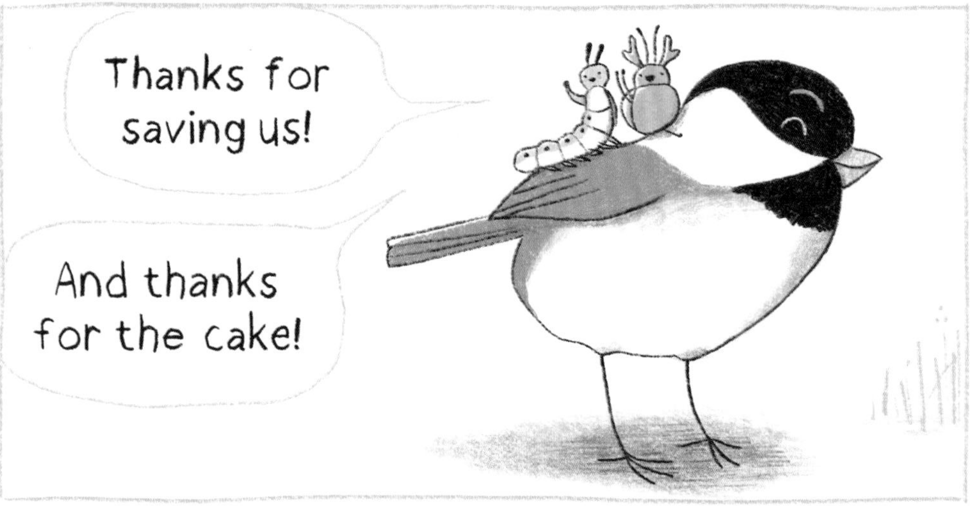
Thanks for saving us!
And thanks for the cake!

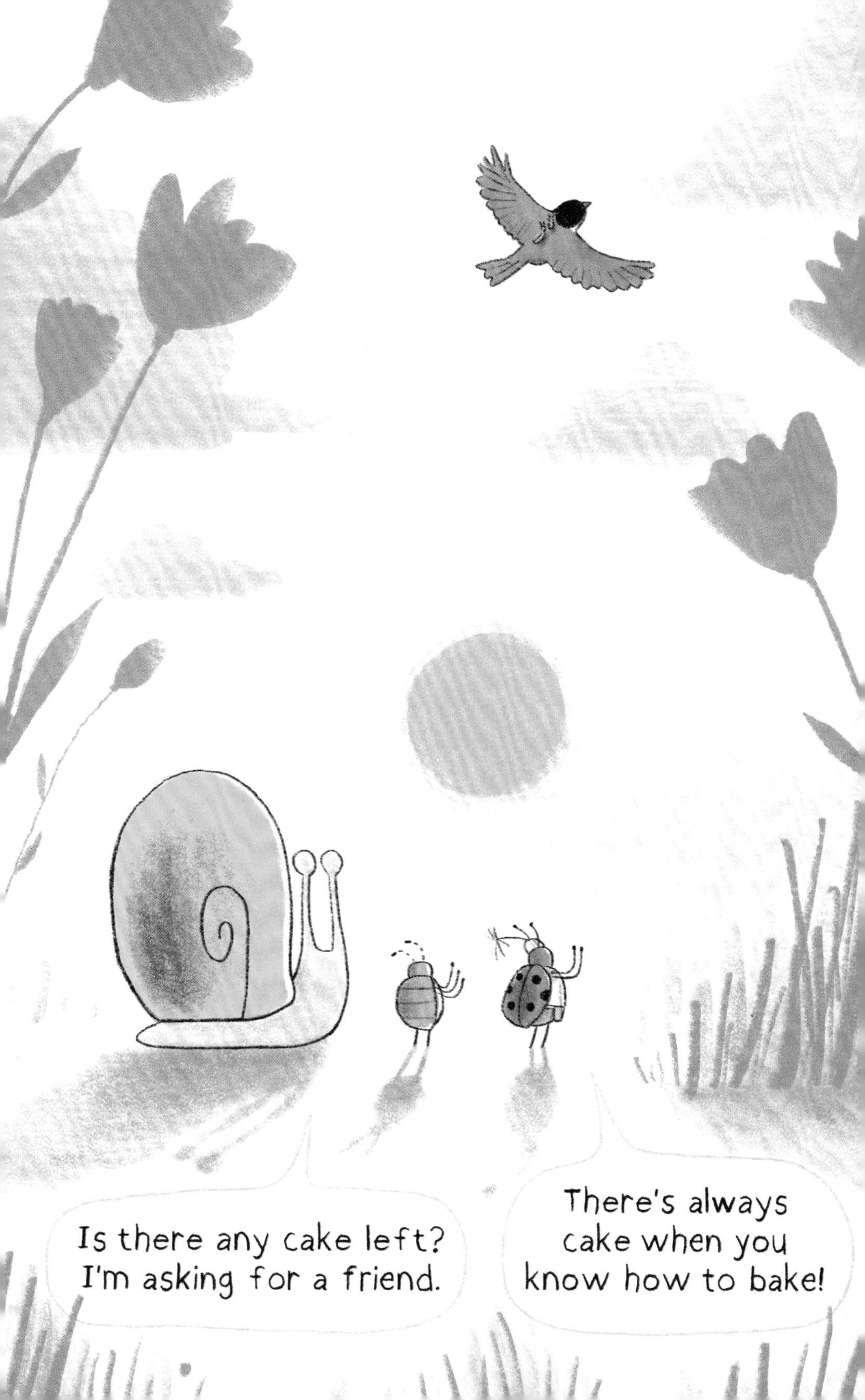
Is there any cake left? I'm asking for a friend.
There's always cake when you know how to bake!

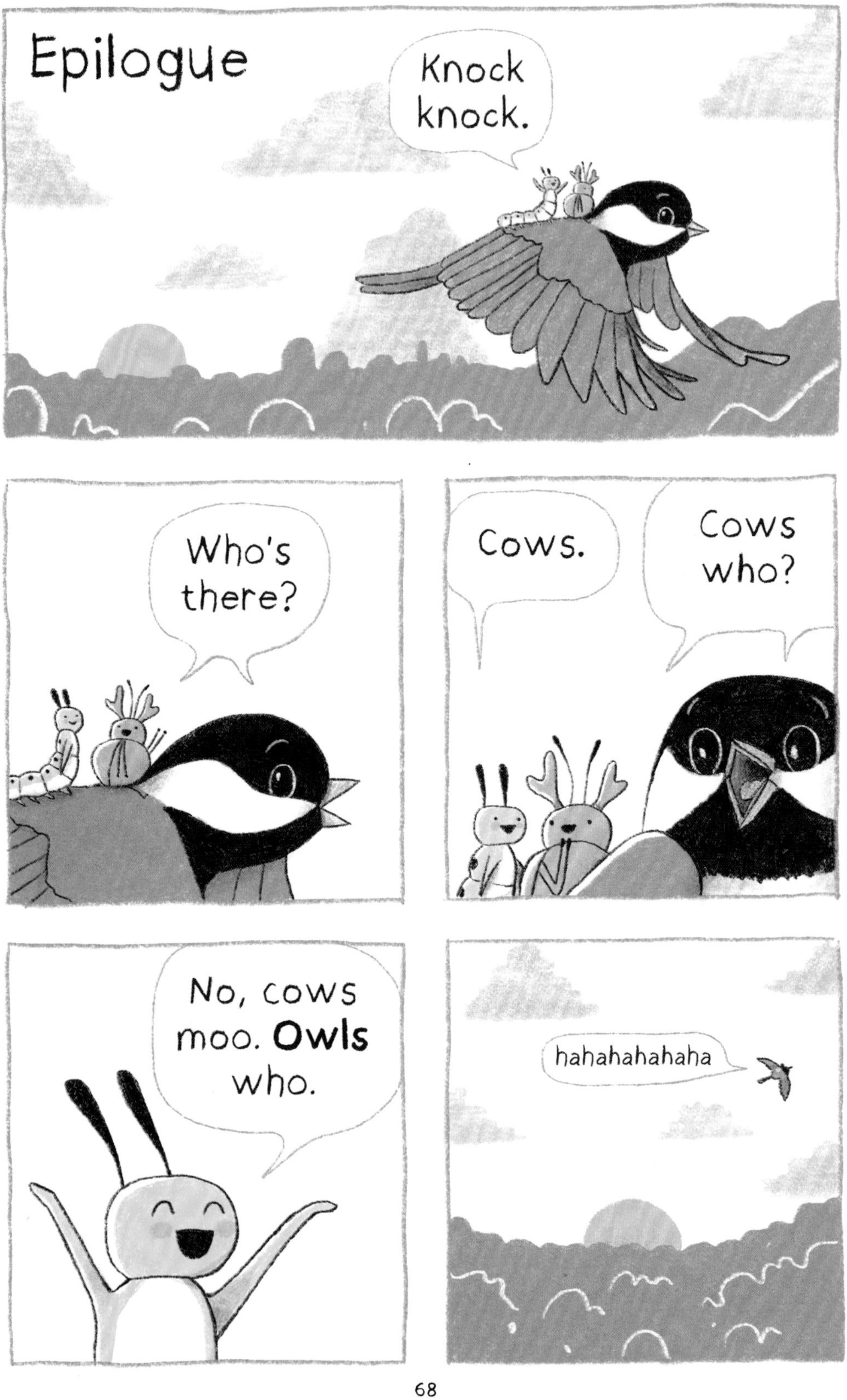
Epilogue
Knock knock.
Who's there?
Cows.
Cows who?
No, cows moo. **Owls** who.
hahahahahaha